LONG
LIVE
the
QUEEN

Magnificent Tales of Misadventure

LONG LIVE the QUEEN

DISCARD

Gerry Swallow

illustrations by Valerio Fabbretti

BLOOMSBURY
NEW YORK LONDON OXFORD NEW DELHI SYDNEY

First published in the United States of America in January 2017
by Bloomsbury Children's Books
www.bloomsbury.com

Bloomsbury is a registered trademark of Bloomsbury Publishing Plc

For information about permission to reproduce selections from this book, write to
Permissions, Bloomsbury Children's Books, 1385 Broadway, New York, New York 10018
Bloomsbury books may be purchased for business or promotional use. For information
on bulk purchases please contact Macmillan Corporate and Premium Sales Department at
specialmarkets@macmillan.com

Library of Congress Cataloging-in-Publication Data
Names: Swallow, Gerry, author. | Fabbretti, Valerio, illustrator.
Title: Long live the queen : magnificent tales of misadventure /
by Gerry Swallow ; illustrations by Valerio Fabbretti.
Description: New York : Bloomsbury, 2017.
Summary: For Elspeth Pule, life is dull and lonely in the real world, where she misses her
good friends Humpty Dumpty, Bo-Peep, and Rodney, a giant, talking wheel of cheese. After
holding her breath until she is blue in the face, Elspeth opens her eyes and finds herself
back in a land where storybook characters are real. Can Elspeth use her bravery, smarts,
and just a little bit of ill temper to thwart the evil witch and rescue her friend Queen Farrah?
Identifiers: LCCN 2016023126 (print) | LCCN 2016036825 (e-book)
ISBN 978-1-61963-490-9 (hardcover) • ISBN 978-1-61963-491-6 (e-book)
Subjects: | CYAC: Behavior—Fiction. | Characters in literature—Fiction. | Fantasy. |
Humorous stories. | BISAC: JUVENILE FICTION / Fantasy & Magic. | JUVENILE FICTION /
Nursery Rhymes. | JUVENILE FICTION / Humorous Stories.
Classification: LCC PZ7.1.S925 Lo 2017 (print) | LCC PZ7.1.S925 (e-book) | DDC [Fic]—dc23
LC record available at https://lccn.loc.gov/2016023126

Book design by Yelena Safronova
Typeset by Newgen Knowledge Works (P) Ltd., Chennai, India
Printed and bound in the U.S.A. by Berryville Graphics Inc., Berryville, Virginia
2 4 6 8 10 9 7 5 3 1

All papers used by Bloomsbury Publishing, Inc., are natural, recyclable products
made from wood grown in well-managed forests. The manufacturing processes
conform to the environmental regulations of the country of origin.

For Ruth

LONG

LIVE

the

QUEEN

Chapter 1

Elspeth hated school, and the idea of returning to it in less than a week was unbearable. How could she go back to such a tedious place after a summer of frequent and wonderful trips to New Winkieland, where she had argued with rocks, made friends with a blabbermouth stick, and had witnessed a pillow fight between two pillows named Andy and Kyle? (Not that it matters, but Andy won by technical knockout.)

You see, in New Winkieland, just about everything—from sticks to shrubs to pillows—is alive. And once school started, Elspeth would have to curtail her visits to this magical place to which she traveled by means of holding her breath until she passed out. Each time she awoke to find herself in the land of Humpty Dumpty, Little Bo-Peep, Georgie Porgie, and the Cheese. You know, the one so very fond of standing alone.

1

In New Winkieland, Elspeth had made the kind of friends she had never been able to in her own world. Dumpty referred to Elspeth's world as the Deadlands, because it was simply that by comparison—dead, as lifeless and devoid of spark as any of her teachers at school. For instance, Elspeth felt convinced that there were B-movie robots with a greater capacity for voice inflection than her Advanced English teacher, Mrs. Weed. And then there was Mr. Evans, the P.E. teacher, who smelled of stale cigars and was so out of shape he used a whistle app on his smartphone, being that he lacked the energy and lung capacity to operate an actual whistle.

Yes, Elspeth hated school. Yet here she was, preparing for the start of another academic year by engaging in one of her least favorite activities: back-to-school shopping at the mall, which seemed to be an annual exercise in determining just how badly her mother could embarrass her by using words that no longer exist.

"Here," Delores Pule said, using her thin, brittle-looking fingers to hold up a pair of jeans from the forty-percent-off rack. "Try on these dungarees. They're on sale."

"Mom," pleaded Elspeth in the kind of harsh whisper that can only be delivered by a mortified twelve-year-old. She nervously scanned the store for anyone she might know. "They're jeans, not dungarees."

"You know what I mean. Now try them on while I go take a look at the sneakers."

Sneakers? Dungarees? How old was her mom? A million?

Actually, Delores, with her rigid posture, poofy, cotton-candy-like hair, and frequent use of outdated phrases, *was* quite a bit older than the mothers of Elspeth's classmates. It was only after Delores had passed her childbearing years that she and her husband, Sheldon, decided to try adoption, a process that proved to be highly discouraging.

Part of the problem was that Mr. and Mrs. Pule were quite adamant that they wanted a girl. Actually, this was a stipulation that was insisted upon by Mrs. Pule, who had always found boys to be too rambunctious.

"But I think it would be every bit as nice to have a boy," Sheldon once suggested.

"Absolutely not," replied Delores. "They're always running around, knocking things over, and making disgusting noises with their armpits and with other parts of their anatomy. We will wait for a girl and that is that."

And so they waited. Soon four years had gone by, and the Pules considered giving up and instead adopting a puppy or a stretch of highway. Then one day, while Mr. Pule was out of town on business, Delores received a call from a lovely woman at the adoption agency named Mrs. Hubbard. The news was just what they had been waiting for but had practically given up on. The agency had taken in a one-year-old girl, and the Pules just happened to be next on the waiting list.

Two days later, they walked into their apartment toting a precious bundle of joy along with a second bundle full of other stuff you need in order to take care of the first bundle: diapers, miniature jars of mashed peas, earplugs . . .

Sheldon and Delores doted on the child to the point of spoiling her silly, and, despite an astonishing lack of physical resemblance between Elspeth and the Pules, the girl grew up believing that Sheldon and Delores were her birth parents. And though they insisted they had fully intended on telling her the truth once she'd turned twelve, Elspeth wasn't so sure that she would have found out if she hadn't encountered her actual birth parents, quite by coincidence, while visiting New Winkieland.

It's one thing to find out you've been adopted by way of accidentally running into your biological mother and father and quite another to discover that they are people you've always thought to be fictional characters. Imagine, for instance, learning that you are the son of Romeo and Juliet or the daughter of Mary Poppins and Zeus. (Not likely as, to my knowledge, the two never dated.)

In Elspeth's case, she initially struggled with the idea before coming to terms with the fact that her real parents were Jack and Jill—two people known to the world mostly for their inability to successfully negotiate a hill while carrying a bucket of water.

As unlikely as the whole thing might have seemed, Elspeth suddenly found herself with two sets of parents: one with whom she lived in the greater Seattle area and another who resided, hidden from the "real world," in the land of nursery rhymes, known once again as New Winkieland now that Elspeth had helped restore Wee Willie Winkie to his rightful place upon the throne while casting out the horrible King Krool.

She was reliving that moment now as she stood in the changing room surrounded by so many angled mirrors that she could actually see the back of her own head, which ached with boredom and an intense longing for the wild exhilaration that could only be had by leading an armed rebellion against an evil tyrant.

Here in the Deadlands, Elspeth was just another middle schooler, destined for a middling life of great inconsequence and staggering mediocrity. But in New Winkieland she was a legend. In fact, during her most recent visit several weeks ago, she was both flattered and slightly embarrassed that King William the Umpteenth had commissioned a statue of her likeness to be erected in the castle courtyard.

"They're a little big around the middle," said Delores, tugging at the waistband of the sale-priced jeans and pulling Elspeth out of the daydream and back to the

Deadlands. "You could wear a belt with them. I think it would look very sharp."

"Sharp?" said Elspeth, staring blankly at the back of her head.

"Yes. You know, snazzy."

Elspeth and her mother left the mall and walked out into a rain-soaked parking lot with two pairs of snazzy dungarees (jeans), two pairs of slacks (pants), a pair of sneakers (tennis shoes), and six new pairs of skivvies (underwear). This rather unimpressive haul had more or less exhausted Elspeth's back-to-school clothing budget. The Pules were not wealthy by any means. In fact, you would be hard pressed to call them middle class. Sheldon Pule was employed as a door-to-door hearing aid salesman while her mother worked from home part-time preparing other people's tax returns.

That home was in a small, four-story apartment building covered in white stucco and dotted with small outcroppings of concrete and iron that were barely big enough to be called balconies, but were anyway, and were crammed with barbecues, bicycles, and a host of other odds and ends.

From her pocket, Elspeth fished out her set of keys, which included one for the main door to the building, one for the door to the apartment, and a mail key. Having keys of her own still held a certain novelty, since she'd only been given them upon turning twelve several months before. And though she rarely went anywhere without at least one of her parents, the keys were symbolic of the fact that she now could if she wanted to.

She held the door open for her mother, and in they went. The interior of the building smelled exactly as you might expect just by looking at it, though perhaps a bit more on the cabbagey side thanks to an old German couple who had moved in next door to the Pules.

And when Elspeth unlocked the door to apartment 207 and she and her mother walked in, they found it to be more cabbagey than usual and especially quiet. Elspeth's father was currently at the other corner of the country, in Florida, attending the annual convention of Worldwide Hearing Aid Traders (also known as WHAT?), where he was due to receive a special award for twenty years of dedicated service.

"What's the matter, dear?" asked Delores. It was a question she had posed frequently to her daughter in recent months: a question that Elspeth had answered in identical fashion each time.

"Nothing. Everything is just fine."

But that's exactly what was the matter. Everything was just fine, which is just dandy if *just fine* is what you strive to be. And though there was a time when Elspeth considered *just fine* to be a perfectly adequate way of feeling, that had all changed now that she'd discovered a world so full of life and so ripe for adventure.

To feel fine was akin to feeling nothing at all as she did now, walking into the small apartment where everything was just as drab and predictable as when she had left it two and a half hours before. There was the coffee table that still featured a small bit of Elspeth's golden hair—stuck between the wooden frame and the glass top—as a result of Elspeth passing out and smacking her head on it.

And though the collision had left a good-size lump on her forehead that remained for weeks, the coffee table had absolutely nothing to say about the encounter and simply went about its business, resting lifelessly in front of the couch, which apparently had no opinion whatsoever as to people sitting upon it.

Yes, everything seemed to be just as it always was. And it continued to seem that way until Elspeth walked into her bedroom and heard the squishing sound and felt the cold water seep in through the sides of her old "sneakers."

The sound and the sensation startled her, but not to the extent that one might think. Though it hadn't happened in quite a while, this was not the first time a puddle of water had appeared on her bedroom floor.

Once thought to be the result of a plumbing problem originating in the apartment above, Elspeth had since solved the mystery of the recurring puddle (which may or may not be the title of a Nancy Drew book Elspeth had once read). As it turns out, every magical kingdom that has a way in must also have a way out, and the way out of New Winkieland just happened to be at the bottom of an abandoned well.

The passageway had been discovered by none other than Jack and Jill, who, upon finding it, had used it on a regular basis to enter the Deadlands for a chance to look upon their precious daughter as she slept, each time leaving a sizable splash of water on the bedroom floor until the carpet became discolored and mildewed.

"I need you to try on these galoshes to see if they still fit," said Delores, appearing in Elspeth's doorway and holding a pair of what most people born in the last century would call boots.

"Great. Here we go again," Delores scoffed, when she saw that her daughter was standing in the middle of a puddle in the middle of her bedroom. "I thought we had this problem all taken care of. Well, I'll have to go find Mr. Droughns and tell him the leak has returned."

"Sure," said Elspeth, distracted by the knowledge that her biological mother and father had been in her room quite recently. Immediately, Elspeth began to worry. After all, this was the first time Jack and Jill had come to visit her in midday. Before now, it was always between midnight and early dawn. So why were they suddenly willing to risk being seen in the light of day? After all, if Delores had walked in on them she would have immediately called the police, who, most likely, would have had a very hard time believing any explanation Elspeth might provide.

"Yes, Officers. It's all very simple. You see, these are my real parents, Jack and Jill. You know, the ones who went up the hill to fetch a pail of water? Anyway, they did not break into the apartment. They arrived here quite legally from the magical kingdom of New Winkieland by way of a secret passage at the bottom of a well."

"I see. Well, thank you, young lady. That certainly explains everything. Have a good day."

Delores went off to find Mr. Droughns, the building superintendent, and Elspeth plopped down upon her bed. She picked up her plastic fashion doll, the one her parents had bought for her to replace the one she'd lost. She had yet to give it a name. What was the point? It was just a doll. As Elspeth looked into its unflinching eyes and ran her fingers down its long auburn hair, more than ever she missed Farrah, who would never visit her in the Deadlands for fear that she might turn back into a lifeless plastic toy like the one Elspeth now held.

She let out a deep sigh, and that sigh quickly turned to a scream when she felt a light tapping upon her ankle.

She jumped to her feet, causing the doll to fly from her vanishing lap and tumble to the floor very near the puddle. She spun around quickly to find, poking out from beneath the bed, a stick. And not just any stick.

"Guess who?" said the skinny, gray stick with a broad smile.

"Gene," gasped Elspeth. "What are you doing here?"

"You'll never guess in a million years."

It's raining, it's pouring,
the Deadlands is boring.
Sat on my bed, a stick then said,
"I come with news and a warning."

Chapter 2

That Gene was here in the Deadlands, still alive and as gabby as ever, gave Elspeth hope. Perhaps Farrah, too, could one day return for a visit without reverting to a lifeless state. Then again, Gene was originally from New Winkieland and had never been anything but alive and insufferably chatty.

And despite having the ability to speak, a walking stick in New Winkieland is no different than a walking stick in the Deadlands. Neither can actually walk, which means that Gene had to have gotten where he was with some help. Sure enough, there soon came a muffled grunt from under the bed.

"Pardon me. Would you mind?"

A hand emerged from the darkness. Elspeth reached down, took the hand, and tugged. She leaned back and pulled on it until a tall, thin man slid out from beneath the bed. The man was Georgie Porgie, also known as King William's chancellor and Chief Secretary of Puddin' and Pie.

"Georgie." Elspeth beamed. "What a surprise."

Georgie took Gene in his other hand, jammed the stick into the carpet like an astronaut planting a flag on the surface of the moon, and, with a grunt, pushed his lanky frame to its feet.

"Hey, easy!" protested Gene. "I'm a stick, not a handrail."

"Sorry," said Georgie, using his stickless hand to brush off the front of his puffy white shirt. Apparently Delores had been far too busy in recent weeks preparing taxes and looking for back-to-school bargains to find time to vacuum under Elspeth's bed because Georgie was positively covered in dust. In fact, clinging to his thin, yellow mustache were a couple of those bunnies of the dust variety.

"You've got something right there," said Elspeth, touching the part of her face that might feature a mustache if she had been able to grow one and had been inclined to do so.

Georgie quickly wiped the small clumps of dust from his face. With a look of disgust, he shook them from his hand. They floated peacefully to the floor like snowflakes, except that, unlike snowflakes, scientists cannot say with absolute certainty that no two dust bunnies are alike.

14

"How long have you been hiding under there?" asked Elspeth.

"Not sure," said Georgie. "My watch stopped working when I jumped into the well." He held his wrist to his ear to see if anything had changed since he last checked his waterlogged watch.

"And why are you here?" Elspeth urged. "Is something wrong?"

"Is something wrong?" said Gene. "That would be the understatement of the century."

Georgie glared down at Gene. "Do you mind? The king has entrusted me with the dissemination of this news, which should be delivered with tact and decorum, two things you seem to be completely without."

"Ha!" scoffed Gene. "I have more tact in my left knothole than you have in your entire body."

"Well, that's classy," said Georgie.

"I am one slick stick," Gene said proudly.

"What is it?" Elspeth persisted. "Is it Jack? Is he okay?"

That Elspeth would make such an assumption was not surprising. After all Jack was a large man with little regard for his own well-being when it came to diet and exercise. His idea of health food was a hot dog in a whole wheat bun or bacon grease that had been freshly squeezed.

"He's fine," said Georgie, bringing Elspeth a measure of relief that would not last long. "I've come here on official royal business."

15

"*You've* come here?" Gene said with a deliberate clearing of his throat. "Seriously. Sometimes I wonder why I even bother."

"Okay," Georgie reluctantly agreed. "*We've* come here on official royal business. It's about Queen Farrah."

"Farrah?" Elspeth repeated. "Is there something the matter with her?"

Farrah was more to Elspeth than just the queen of New Winkieland. She had, for years, been Elspeth's favorite toy and closest confidante. It was only upon leaving the Deadlands behind that the former fashion doll had become sentient: a walking, talking, living, breathing miniature person. Not long after her arrival, her beauty and charm had captured the heart of the similarly tiny Wee Willie Winkie, also known as King William the Umpteenth.

"I'm afraid," said Georgie, "that Her Majesty has been kidnapped."

"What?" Elspeth gasped. The news was indeed alarming. "Kidnapped? By whom?"

"By Mary Mary," Georgie replied.

Elspeth had only ever heard of two people with a double first name. One of them was a boy named John John who used to be in her class but was now being homeschooled. "You mean Mary Mary Quite Contrary?"

"Contrary indeed," Gene spat. "That's the nicest thing anyone has ever said about her, I can guarantee you that. More like Mary Mary incredibly scary. Or Mary Mary better be wary. Or Mary Mary she's got a big fat hairy . . ."

"Okay, you've painted quite a vivid picture," Georgie interrupted. "She is quite hideous to be sure."

"And she smells awful," said Gene. "Seriously, would it kill her to take a bath once in a while?"

Elspeth had become accustomed to hearing about nursery rhyme characters who were not quite what she had always known them to be. Old King Cole turned out to be the evil King Krool and anything but a merry old soul. Little Bo-Peep was not so little and hadn't lost her sheep but had had them stolen away from her and eaten by Krool himself. And the Owl and the Pussycat's beautiful pea-green boat had been the target of a torpedo attack, which resulted in making a widower of Fergus, the poor old owl.

And now Mary Mary Quite Contrary apparently had things on her mind other than tending to her garden of silver bells and cockleshells. "But why would she want to kidnap Queen Farrah?"

"Money. Why else?" said Gene. "The king found one of the queen's shoes, along with a ransom note demanding one million sixpence."

"So you mean six million pence, then," said Elspeth.

"No," said Gene. "Read my wooden lips. One million sixpence."

"King William is beside himself with worry and grief," said Georgie, who had taken to pacing the room nervously, tapping Gene repeatedly on the carpet as he did. "After years of Krool upon the throne, living in extravagance, the royal coffers are quite empty. If we don't meet her demands by the deadline, she's vowed to turn the queen into a muskrat."

"That's horrible," said Elspeth.

"Oh, you have no idea," said Gene. "King William is incredibly allergic to musk."

"But turning someone into a muskrat? I mean, can she do that?" asked Elspeth.

"You mean legally or practically?" said Gene.

"If what you're asking is whether she's capable of such a thing, the answer is, I don't know for sure," said Georgie. "But it's best not to test her. After all, she is a very powerful witch."

"Mary Mary Quite Contrary is a witch?" asked Elspeth.

"How did you think she was able to grow cockleshells in a garden?" answered Gene. "She apparently also had quite a nice harvest of mussels this year and a bumper crop of clams."

"Well, this is all very horrible," said Elspeth, because she could think of nothing more useful to say. "When is the deadline?"

"Sunday at noon, New Winkieland time," said Georgie. "So you can imagine how desperate the king is for your assistance in the matter."

"I'm not sure what I can do," said Elspeth. "I've got about eighty dollars in a savings account. No idea how many sixpence that's worth, but probably not a million."

"The king would never dream of taking your money," replied Georgie. "What he needs is your guidance. Your leadership."

"Your ability to kick some butt," added Gene.

"Nice," said Georgie.

"What can I say?" Gene gloated.

"Well, of course I'll help in whatever way I can," said Elspeth.

"Just so you know," said Gene, "it's bound to be dangerous."

Gene's disclaimer did little to dissuade Elspeth. A bit of danger might be just what she needed to snap her out of the funk she'd been in for weeks. "Okay," she said. "But we'd better get going right away. School starts on Monday."

As she grabbed her jacket from the closet and slipped it on, the sudden sounds of Delores and Mr. Droughns entering the apartment sent everyone into a general and immediate state of panic. Georgie gasped and brought his hands to his face, dropping Gene to the floor in the process.

"Hey," Gene protested.

"Shh!" Elspeth admonished.

As voices grew louder and footsteps closer, Elspeth rushed to the door and slammed it shut, pressing her back firmly against it.

"Quick," she hissed, much in the same way she had at her mother while shopping at the mall. "You've got to hide."

Georgie immediately unfroze himself and dropped to the floor.

"No," said Elspeth. "They might see you under there while they're checking the puddle. In the closet."

Georgie crawled across the room and into the closet, closing the door behind him just as there came a knock upon the door to Elspeth's room.

"Hello?" her mother called. "Elspeth? Are you in there? I'm here with Mr. Droughns."

"Hold on," Elspeth replied in what she hoped sounded like a normal tone. "I was just trying on my new dungarees. To see how they look with my new sneakers. I'll be right there."

She shuffled across the room, scooped up the dust bunnies, and stuffed them into her pocket. Then she picked up Gene, walked back to the door, and opened it to reveal her mother standing next to Mr. Droughns, his hair plugs looking more than ever like a patch of dry crabgrass.

"Well?" asked Delores. "How did you find them?"

"Find who?" asked Elspeth, her heart thumping almost visibly through her shirt.

"Not who. What. Your dungarees with your sneakers? How did you find they look together?"

"Oh. Very sharp. Downright snazzy."

"I knew they would."

"Excuse me," said the temporarily forgotten Mr. Droughns. "I'm awfully busy this morning."

"Right," said Delores. "So sorry. It's over here. In the usual spot."

Elspeth stepped aside, and Delores led the short, stocky building superintendent to the puddle. He looked at it for a moment before applying the toe of his shoe to it, perhaps to test its degree of gooshiness.

Delores bent down and picked up Elspeth's new fashion doll. "Elspeth," she said. "How many times have I told you not to leave your things on the floor? These dolls are not cheap, you know."

"Sorry," said Elspeth. Delores placed the doll in a sitting position upon the tidy dresser next to a small collection of Elspeth's chess tournament trophies. Mr. Droughns clamped his hands to his hips and stared blankly at the ceiling for such a long time that the silence became awkward.

"Perhaps it's coming from the apartment below," Delores offered.

This caused Mr. Droughns to remove his blank gaze from the ceiling and cast an even blanker one at Delores. "You're suggesting that maybe there's water running *up* from the apartment below?"

"It's possible, isn't it?"

"No," said Mr. Droughns flatly, as if he couldn't quite be sure whether Delores was joking. "Not possible."

"Are you sure?"

"Have you ever heard of a river running uphill?"

"I suppose not." Delores sighed. "Well then, I'm out of ideas."

"So am I," said Mr. Droughns. "Now if you'll excuse me, apartment 305 is complaining about a cabbagey smell."

"But what shall we do about the puddle?" asked Delores.

"Get a couple of goldfish," said Droughns as he turned and made his way out of the apartment.

"Well," said Delores. "He wasn't much help at all, was he?" Then, glancing down at Elspeth's hand, she added, "And what on earth are you doing with that filthy stick?"

Elspeth bit her lip and held her breath. Gene wasn't one to endure such insults without a counterattack. She gave the stick a quick squeeze as a way to plead with him to remain silent.

"Oh, this?" said Elspeth. "Found it outside."

"Well, can you put it back outside? I don't want any dirty old sticks in the house."

Elspeth could feel Gene bristling beneath her grip, and she gave him a harder squeeze, this time more as a warning to keep his mouth shut. "Sure," Elspeth agreed. "I'll do it later, if you don't mind. Right now I'm going to have a little nap. All that shopping has left me exhausted."

"I know what you mean," said Delores. "It's a lot of excitement for one day. I can't believe our little girl is going into seventh grade. You've grown up so fast. Well, I'm going to get the house in order. Your father's flight lands in an hour. Have a nice nap."

Delores gave Gene one last disapproving look before walking out of Elspeth's room. No sooner had Elspeth closed the door behind her mother than Gene decided he could no longer contain himself.

"Dirty old stick?" he blurted out. "Did you hear that? I've got half a mind to give her a sharp smack to the head."

"Shh! She'll hear you." Elspeth locked the door, another thing she had only been allowed to do since turning twelve.

"Too bad," said Gene. "And by the way, thanks for coming to my defense." He pouted like only a highly offended stick can. "Oh, this grubby, old, worm-infested thing? Found it outside just lying in the gutter like common driftwood."

"I never said that," Elspeth protested.

"Might as well have," Gene huffed.

"Stop acting like a baby," whispered Elspeth. "We don't have time for this nonsense." She walked across the room and opened the closet door, and out crawled Georgie. "Okay, I got rid of her," said Elspeth. "We're in the clear. Now let's move out."

"See?" said Gene. "That's what I'm talking about right there. Your take-charge, kick-butt attitude."

"Okay," said Georgie, climbing to his feet. "One question. We got here through the well. But how do we get back?"

"Easy," said Elspeth. "Just hold your breath until you pass out. When you come to, you'll be back in New Winkieland. Works every time."

"I don't know," said Gene. "I don't think I can do this. I've never passed out before."

"Not true," said Georgie. "Remember the royal wedding reception?"

"Not much of it," said Gene. "But that's only because the Cheese spiked the punch. You know, I liked him a lot better when he stood alone."

Well practiced in the art of ignoring Gene, Elspeth set him down on the carpet to one side of the puddle. "It's safest if we lie down on the floor first," she explained. "Trust me, you don't want to crack your head open when you lose consciousness."

She lay down next to Gene while Georgie stretched out along the space on the opposite side of the puddle.

"Okay," said Elspeth. "When I count to three, everyone hold your breath and I'll see you on the other side. One, two, three."

Each of them closed his or her eyes, drew in a deep breath, and held it. Ten seconds went by, then twenty, then . . .

"It's not working," said Gene.

Elspeth quickly and angrily exhaled two lungfuls of oxygen-free air.

"Well, it won't work if you're talking," she scolded. "Now get serious. Every second that goes by the queen is closer to being turned into a muskrat. Okay, let's try this again. One, two . . ."

"You know, when I have trouble sleeping I sing a little song my mother used to sing to me," said Gene. "Maybe I should try that and see if it works now. It goes a little bit like this: 'My precious Gene, with leaf of green, please go to sleeeeeep, before I scream.'"

"Three," said Elspeth as she reached out and clamped her hand over Gene's nose and mouth. She closed her eyes, held her breath, and the last thing she remembered hearing were the muffled protests of a blathering stick with the complete inability to carry a tune.

Diddle, diddle, dumpling, my queen's gone,
Captured by a wicked pawn;
One shoe off, and one shoe on,
Diddle, diddle, dumpling, my queen's gone.

Chapter
3

It's not every day that you can exhale a lungful of air that smells of mildew, cabbage, and dust bunnies and immediately take in one that's alive with the aromas of fir and willow trees and rich, moist earth. Once a person who despised the outdoors, Elspeth had since developed a full appreciation of the forest and all the beauty it offered. She opened her eyes and, for a moment, just gazed upward at a patch of blue sky, visible through the emergent trees. Slowly, she turned her head to see Georgie lying next to her, just coming to as well.

"We made it," he said with a smile of surprise and relief.

"Don't sit up right away," Elspeth cautioned. "I've found it's best to give your brain a chance to come around a bit."

Whether it was beneficial or not, lying completely still and perfectly silent gave Elspeth the opportunity to listen to all the soothing sounds of the woods. There were birds chirping, crickets cricketing, and leaves rustling. It took but a few seconds to realize that of all the sounds Elspeth expected to hear, there was one that she did not.

"Gene!" She'd completely forgotten to remove her hand from his mouth and nose. When she finally did, the stick fell to the ground, lying motionless and utterly failing to respond to Elspeth's repeated pleas for him to snap out of it.

"Oh no," she cried. "What have I done?" Elspeth reached out and grabbed Georgie quite roughly by his puffy shirt. "Don't just sit there. Do something."

"Such as?"

"Such as anything! Do you know mouth-to-mouth?"

"As King William's chancellor it's a job requirement, but . . ."

"But what?"

"You want me to give mouth-to-mouth to a stick?" Elspeth said nothing in reply. Her piercing glare conveyed her thoughts loudly and clearly. "Okay, okay. I'll do it," Georgie conceded.

He knelt over the unconscious stick, let out a shudder, and then brought his lips to Gene's. He delivered a breath of air and then another and then a third. It wasn't until the ninth blast of air that Gene began coughing, sputtering, and finally breathing on his own.

"You did it!" Elspeth cheered. "You saved his life!"

"Yes, I suppose I did," said Georgie, wiping his mouth with the puffy sleeve of his puffy shirt. "Is there any bark in my teeth?"

"No," said Elspeth, making no effort to hide the fact that she had just lost a little respect for Georgie. "Your precious teeth are just fine."

When Gene's coughing fit had subsided, he blinked several times and looked up at Georgie through dilated pupils. "Mom? Is that you?"

"What? I'm not your mother. Do I look like a stick to you? It's me. Georgie. And we're back in New Winkieland."

"Will you sing me a song?" Gene purred.

"No, I will not sing you a song," snapped Georgie.

"Gene," said Elspeth. "Don't you recognize us? It's your old friend Elspeth."

Gene scrunched his eyes shut and kept them that way for a moment before snapping them back open. Elspeth was relieved to see a smile spread across his tiny wooden face. "Hey," he said. "I know you guys."

"We were worried that maybe we'd lost you," said Elspeth. "I'm sorry. I'm sorry I put you through that."

"Oh, I don't know," said Gene. "Wasn't so bad. Certainly easier than going the other way. Just try swimming to the bottom of a well when you're made of wood.

No simple task, even for a stick of my considerable talents."

Elspeth smiled. Despite having nearly been suffocated to death, there was certainly nothing wrong with Gene.

Elspeth plucked the gabby stick from the ground and stood up, as did Georgie. They brushed dirt and leaves from their clothing, and because they all knew the way to the castle, they simply began walking in that direction. The route would take them to the edge of the forest, across Torcano Alley, up the red cliffs at the other end, and over the rolling, grassy hills to the town of Banbury Cross, nestled in the shadow of the great castle with its gleaming white towers and red-tile roofs.

"So how did it happen?" asked Elspeth as they wound their way along the path with which Elspeth had become quite familiar. "How was Mary Mary able to kidnap the queen?"

"By appealing to her kind heart and good nature," Georgie explained. "And with good old-fashioned treachery."

"That's right," Gene chimed in. "Mary Mary isn't only a witch. She's a mog."

"Mog? I'm afraid I'm not familiar with the word," Elspeth admitted.

"A mog is someone with the ability to take on various forms," said Georgie. "That's how she was able to coax the queen from within the safety of the castle walls. By appearing as an injured kitten."

"Oh, I see," said Elspeth. "Mog. It comes from 'transmogrify.'"

"Actually," said Gene. "Nobody knows where they come from."

"But we do know that Mary Mary resides in the Thick," added Georgie, "which is where she is holding the queen captive. And where she's insisted the delivery of the ransom be made."

"The Thick" was a term well known to Elspeth, being that it was the name given by the locals to the deepest, darkest part of the forest, said to be home to savage beasts, including but not limited to: the Germese Stranglerat, the poisonous tiger snake, the Great Spiny Gleekin, and, apparently, mogs.

"Well, that certainly complicates things," said Elspeth. "I mean, in terms of mounting a rescue effort."

"A rescue effort?" said Georgie. "Certainly you're not suggesting King William defy Mary Mary's demands when she holds the queen's life in her hands."

"What she's demanding is something we don't have, so we've really got no choice, as I see it," said Elspeth.

"I've been thinking that perhaps we could raise the money," Georgie offered.

"Raise six million pence by Sunday? Just exactly what did you have in mind?"

"Oh, I don't know," said Georgie, suddenly very disinterested in making eye contact. "Haven't really thought about it."

"Tell her," said Gene.

"Stay out of this," snapped Georgie.

"A bake sale," said Gene with a snicker. "That's his great plan. To raise one million sixpence with a bake sale."

"And a raffle," Georgie snorted.

"How about a lemonade stand?" Gene taunted. "Have you thought of that?"

"Maybe. Anyway, I don't see you coming up with better ideas."

"Oh, I've got plenty of ideas, you can count on that," said Gene. "Still working out the details, that's all."

The bickering continued until it became nothing more than noise to Elspeth and the drone ceased only when they happened upon an old friend, standing just off the path.

"Hola, señorita," said Manuel, a sprawling willow tree whose plentiful leaves had at one time provided cover for the encampment that Elspeth's friends had been forced to call home. "Good to see you."

"It's good to see you, too, Manuel." Elspeth gave the tree a hug, and Manuel responded by wrapping his branches around her.

"It gets pretty lonely out here since everybody left," he said. "I wish you could come by more often."

"So do I," said Elspeth. "And I wish I could stay and chat. But in case you haven't heard, the queen's been kidnapped by Mary Mary and taken off to the Thick."

If trees had knees, Manuel's would surely have buckled at the news. "That is most terrible," he said. "If there's anything I can do—"

"Perhaps you could send a message across the forest and into the Thick," said Georgie. "It would be helpful to know if any of the trees there have seen her."

"I can try," said Manuel. "But those trees in the Thick are not like those of us here. Like Mary Mary herself, they're not to be trusted."

With a promise to give his best regards to all in Banbury Cross, Elspeth bid Manuel good-bye, and she and the others continued down the path until they stepped out onto the dry plain of Torcano Alley, so called for the fact that it was a hot spot for torcanoes—a combination tornado/volcano that could appear at a moment's notice and sweep across the land at an alarming speed, destroying all in its path.

The earth along this stretch was scarred with wide, magma-filled crevasses from which the torcano would arm itself by pulling up the molten rock with its powerful vortex. On her initial visit to New Winkieland, Elspeth had nearly been killed by a torcano, not once but twice.

It sure would be helpful, she thought, if she could enter New Winkieland somewhat closer to the castle, but instead she arrived each time in the middle of the forest, on the far side of Torcano Alley.

The three travelers stood for a moment, looking left, then right like children preparing to cross a busy street. It was an exercise in futility considering the miles-wide expanse of the plain and the speed with which a torcano can appear, completely independent of atmospheric conditions and regardless of whether you really hope that it won't.

"Should be okay," said Georgie, more to himself than to the others. "It's nearing the end of the heavy season. All the same, we'd better make haste."

Zigzagging around the wider cracks and skipping over the narrower, they made good time. Gene's horrible singing served to distract them from the possibility of a worse fate.

In just over an hour they crossed the alley without the slightest hint of a torcano and now had only to scale the switchback trail of the red cliffs to be completely out of danger, at least as it pertained to lava-filled tornadoes.

Whereas a path through a forest grows more passable with repeated use, a switchback trail up a cliff made of dry, crumbly dirt becomes less so as wind, rain, the occasional torcano, and the drag of heavy, tired feet eat away at it bit by bit. The path had eroded and narrowed so much that Elspeth was thankful to have a walking stick, even one that had finally stopped singing and had suddenly begun rapping instead.

"My name is Gene. Yo. I'm long and lean. Yo. I've got heart, but I haven't got a spleen. Whoa."

"Something's just now occurred to me," grunted Georgie as he struggled to keep up with his much younger traveling companion. "Those brief few moments when he was unconscious were among the happiest of my life."

"Some people have no appreciation for the arts," Gene retorted.

"Not true," said Georgie. "For instance, I love wood carving."

"That's not helpful, Georgie," Elspeth called back. Although to Georgie's way of thinking it had been immensely helpful in that it had put a sudden end to the rapping. A pouting stick was a quiet stick.

Elspeth reached the top of the cliff and straightened up. Looking in the direction of the castle, she was glad to be greeted by a most pleasing sight. It was Fergus. With his full wingspan on display, the great horned owl made an impressive stamp upon a cloudless sky.

With a whoosh of displaced air, he glided down toward an old oak tree named Beatrice. Upon final approach, the bird wobbled and swayed and very nearly missed the branch of his intended landing altogether, barely catching it with the talons of his left foot, his downward momentum taking him to an inverted position where he hung beneath the limb like a large, feathered bat.

"Sorry, Beatrice old girl," said the owl.

"No bark off my limbs," the tree responded.

"Fergus," Elspeth sputtered. "How did you . . . ? I mean, they said . . ."

"Said I would never fly again," Fergus finished as he dropped from the branch and fluttered to the ground at Elspeth's feet. "I guess I showed them a thing or two."

In a selfless attempt to rescue Elspeth from King Krool's dungeon, Fergus had suffered devastating injuries to his left wing by way of a guard's lance—wounds that had left him earthbound and declared unfit for flight.

"Of course," Fergus continued, "I can only turn to the left, which requires a lot of extra circling in the event that I need to turn right. And my landings are still a bit on the rough side."

"Yes, I noticed that," said Elspeth. "Would you like a ride back to the castle?"

"Thank you," said Fergus, and he fluttered up and landed clumsily on Elspeth's right shoulder. From that position, Elspeth could not see his face and the sudden serious look upon it.

"On behalf of the king, thank you for coming," he said. "As you know, the situation is quite dire, and we're grateful for your pledge to help."

"Of course I had to come," said Elspeth. "And don't worry. We'll figure something out."

"I have every confidence in you."

Georgie trudged to the landing and immediately bent forward, resting his hands upon his knees.

"Welcome back, Georgie," Fergus offered. "How did you find the journey?"

"Wet," said Georgie. "And annoying." He punctuated this by casting a glance in Gene's direction.

"I heard that," said Gene.

"Please," Elspeth implored. "We still have a long walk to the castle. And if you could just stop griping at each other, it would give Fergus and I a chance to talk."

"Fergus and *me*," said Fergus, quickly reminding Elspeth that the owl could be both warmly endearing and incredibly tiresome when it came to matters of grammar. "You simply take the other person out of the sentence and . . ."

"Yes, yes," said Elspeth. "I know how it works. I just misspoke, that's all."

"Excuse me," said Gene. "If you two could quit griping at each other it would give Georgie and *me* a chance to talk."

"Oh, quiet," said Elspeth. "Now come on, let's go." She stomped ahead so abruptly that Fergus almost teetered from his perch.

"King William offers his sincerest apologies that he was not able to meet you in person," said the owl. "But since the queen's abduction he barely has the strength to get out of bed in the morning."

"I can imagine how worried he is," said Elspeth. "Truth is, I'm worried too. This Mary Mary sounds like a terrible person."

"You've no idea," said Fergus. "In addition to being quite the embodiment of evil, she has command of all the beasts of the Thick. They do her bidding out of fear."

"You mean the Great Spiny Gleekin is afraid of *her*?"

"And only her. Beyond that, it has no natural enemy. Then again, neither does she."

Mary Mary, spiteful, scary
How do you bring such woe?
With awful smells and wicked spells
And hideous creatures in tow.

Chapter
4

On the day the queen went missing and on every day since, King William had ordered the flag on the castle's East Tower to be flown at half-staff, though on this particularly still afternoon it did little flying and, instead, hung from the flagpole shapeless and slack, words that could easily be used to describe the king himself lately.

"Oh, what's taking them so long?" he wailed as he shuffled about his sleeping chambers, still in his pajamas, his chin prickly with a four-day growth of stubble. The skin of his bald head was chafed from running his hands back and forth across it simply because he knew not what else to do.

Near to the king stood two mice, one brown and one gray, watching him with looks of great concern. As the king's personal attendants, Earl Grey and James Brown had seen, up close, his steady and continual descent into despair. They had seen it up close because, being extremely visually impaired, that's the only way they could see anything.

"What do you think?" James Brown whispered to Earl Grey as Winkie continued his lamentations. "He doesn't look well. Blurrier than usual. Should we call Dr. Foster?"

Winkie fell face-first onto his bed and groaned into his pillow.

"He's already been seen by the doctor," said Earl Grey. "He's given His Highness more pills than Old MacDonald's got pigs. He says there's really nothing more he can do."

"I have another idea," said James Brown. "Pardon me, Your Majesty."

Winkie lifted his face from the pillow and turned his head slowly in James Brown's direction. "What is it?"

"It occurs to me that His Highness is quite distraught. Perhaps a little levity is in order. After all, laughter is the best medicine. Should I summon the court jester?"

"Oh, that's a marvelous idea," said Winkie. He rolled over and sat up quickly. If he had been closer to the mice, they would have seen the unsteady look in his eye. "The love of my life has been kidnapped by an evil witch who has threatened to turn her into a muskrat unless I come up with a million sixpence by Sunday. Let's see, what could possibly cheer me up? Oh, I know. How about a clown juggling bowling pins while riding a unicycle? Yes, that's just the ticket."

James Brown gently cleared his throat. "To the best of my knowledge the jester's unicycle is in the shop," he said. "But I hear he has some new pratfalls that are said to be the absolute height of buffoonery."

"I believe His Majesty was being sarcastic," whispered Earl Grey.

"Of course I was being sarcastic!" said Winkie in a voice quite large for a man the size of a table lamp. He climbed off the bed and walked to the window, looking out across the village and beyond to the forest in the distance. "There's only one thing that's going to cheer me up, and that's the safe return of the queen."

Just then a third mouse, plump and stark white, scurried into the room. "Good news from the sentries, Your Highness," said Barry White. "Lady Elspeth approaches the village."

With another look out the window, Winkie was able to confirm this. There was Elspeth, just passing beyond the wall to the city. Immediately the king began moving with a sense of urgency and a level of energy not seen in days. "Quickly," he said, his demeanor approaching manic. "Get me my shirt. And my pants. And those other things." He snapped his fingers several times, urging his brain to come up with the right word. "You know, the ones you wear on your feet."

"Socks?"

"Yes, socks. Come on now. I can't be expected to receive our honored guest without proper footwear."

The three visually impaired mice rushed to gather the king's pants, shirt, and those things you wear on your feet. They worked frantically to try and make him presentable in the time it would take for Elspeth to walk from the edge of the village, across the drawbridge, and into the castle's throne room.

Though he practically threw on his clothes, Winkie determined there was no time for a shave, so he simply splashed his face with water from a ceramic basin and dried it on the curtains. "There," he said. "How do I look?"

"As though you have your pants on inside out," said Earl Grey.

"And upside down," added James Brown.

"Argh," snarled Winkie, quickly peeling them off and angrily stuffing his legs back into the properly oriented pants. "There. Now how do I look?"

"Like a million sixpence," said Earl Grey.

Like a million sixpence (or six million pence) is the way Elspeth felt each and every time she arrived at Banbury Cross. To be both hailed as a hero and greeted as a friend was the best anyone could ever hope for, she thought. Villagers rushed from their cottages bearing gifts and warm wishes, and soon Elspeth found herself

43

being ushered down the cobblestones and toward the castle like a sailboat pushed along by a breeze of pure joy and enthusiasm. And though she had just arrived, the thought of having to leave again was already weighing heavily upon her. How could she go back to the Deadlands? With so much love and so much life, how could she? Why would she?

Because it was expected of her, that's why. And to remain here would break Delores's and Sheldon's hearts. All parents claim they only want their children to be happy, but few would grant them that happiness at the expense of losing them to a stronger loyalty, or to a world so removed from their own.

Elspeth pushed the thoughts from her head and returned to basking in the adulation of the growing throng while Georgie fell farther behind, cut off by the surging masses. Fergus grew increasingly uncomfortable, and his grip on Elspeth's shoulder was soon tight enough to cause discomfort.

"Easy now," he directed the crowd. "No pushing. Give us some room here."

Many of those who showed up to welcome Elspeth she had never met in person, while others she considered close friends and some, of course, were family.

Jack and Jill stood, side by side and hand in hand, near the castle gate. Though Elspeth could catch only brief glimpses of them among all the waving arms, she could see they were smiling as if they hadn't stopped since the last time she'd seen them. Jill's smile was tight-lipped but warm and soft, and Jack's, like Elspeth's, was wide, gap-toothed, and unabashed.

If it were possible to run to them she would have, but there were too many well-wishers with too many feet to trip over. In addition, autograph seekers shoved pencils and paper into her hands while others thrust babies toward her face so she would kiss them for good luck.

"Please," pleaded Fergus, who was not terribly fond of babies. "Keep that thing to yourself. And refrain from pushing. Make way, I implore you."

"You're being too polite," shouted Gene. "Let me show you how it's done. Hey! Listen up, losers! Big-time celebrities here. VIPs coming through. Audience with the king. Back off."

Gene's less than polite methods proved no more effective, and soon Fergus, feeling claustrophobic and in danger of suffering another wing injury, took to the air. When Elspeth finally reached Jack and Jill she hugged each in turn the way she had tried to hug her parents back home, but that always felt forced and unnatural. Not because she didn't love her adoptive parents. They were wonderful people who had provided her with food, shelter, and the only kind of love they themselves had ever known. It was a brand of love that was cautious and dosed out in carefully measured amounts.

On the other hand, her love for Jack and Jill and theirs for her was, like Jack's smile, unbridled and seemingly limitless, with nothing to get in the way of it. Unlike Delores, Jill seemed to pay little attention to her physical appearance. She wore no makeup, her hair was short and sometimes combed, and her clothing was as rumpled as Delores's was neatly pressed and perfectly matched.

And while Sheldon spent much of his life in the pursuit of money and locked in the doldrums of not having enough of it, Jack was every bit as poor yet seemed to be entirely unbothered by the fact. He worked as a garbage collector and had no career ambitions other than earning a decent living. His wife worked as a nurse, and, standing next to each other, they smelled vaguely of rubbing alcohol and trash.

"You're getting to be quite the celebrity around here," said Jack.

Elspeth rolled her eyes. "If I have to kiss one more baby, I think I'm going to scream."

Jill smiled and held Elspeth at arm's length in order to a have a full look at her daughter. "You've cut your hair," she said. "And you seem so much taller."

"It's only been three weeks," said Elspeth.

"Three weeks in your world," Jack reminded her.

It was true that time in the Deadlands did seem to move much more slowly than it did in New Winkieland. Though Elspeth's first visit here lasted several weeks,

46

upon her return home she discovered she'd only been gone for ten minutes. It was as close as one could get to immortality, cramming weeks of living into mere minutes.

"I'm only sorry it took the queen being kidnapped to bring you back to us once more," said Jill.

"Speaking of which," said Gene, "we should probably keep moving here."

"Yes," agreed Elspeth. "From what I understand, King William is quite beside himself these days."

"At night his sobs can be heard throughout the village," said Jack. "He's an absolute mess."

"Well, how would you feel if someone were to kidnap me and carry me off into the Thick?" Jill asked her husband.

"At first I would feel horrible," said Jack. "Then, after a while, I would feel hungry."

Jack's ample midsection absorbed a sharp backhand from his wife.

"What? I'm just saying that you're such a wonderful cook that I would sooner go hungry than eat something prepared by anyone else."

Jill rolled her eyes before turning them back to Elspeth. "Go," she said. "You don't want to be around to see how this turns out."

How Elspeth wished her other parents had such a playful way with each other!

"Will you have time to come by for supper one night before you return?" asked Jill.

"I hope so," Elspeth replied. "I guess it all depends on how quickly we can get Queen Farrah back safe and sound. But of course I'll do my best."

"Good," said Jack. "Because we've got some important news to share with you."

Again Jill's hand collided with Jack's protruding gut. "Jack, honestly."

"What?" Jack protested.

"You never tell someone you have news to tell them. It causes people to worry, and Elspeth has enough on her mind."

"Should I be worried?" asked Elspeth.

"Of course not," said Jill with a smile that could reassure Elspeth in even the most dire of circumstances.

"Good. Then I'll see you when I get back."

"When you get back from where?" said Jack. "It was my understanding that you were being brought in only as an advisor on this. Surely King William wouldn't ask you to go to the Thick."

"Of course he wouldn't," said Elspeth. "Don't worry so much. I'm not going anywhere near the Thick," she promised before giving them each another quick hug.

Walking across the open drawbridge and into the castle courtyard, the first thing Elspeth noticed, planted directly in the center, surrounded by the various shops, was the statue. In fact, at twelve feet in height, it was quite impossible to miss. When she'd last visited it was only in the planning stages, but now there it was, her very own image, cast in bronze. The figure stood proud and tall, dressed in full military regalia and thrusting a stick high into the air. And not just any stick. The mouths of the two figures, both the girl's and the stick's, were fashioned as if shouting, "Charge!"

"Well?" said Gene. "What do you think? Pretty good likeness, if you ask me."

Elspeth sized it up for a moment. Not bad, she supposed. But something was off. "My eyes are a little too beady," she said.

"I was talking about me," said Gene. "I think they really captured my true essence, don't you?"

"Oh, absolutely," said Elspeth.

"When I found out they were putting a statue of me in the courtyard I insisted that you be included in it," said Gene. "Hope you don't mind."

"Oh, not at all," said Elspeth. "I'm honored to be a small part of your great contribution to society."

Though Elspeth may have made light of it, secretly she was feeling quite pleased with herself. She stood in the statue's considerable shadow for a few moments before she sensed an additional presence nearby.

"You're right," came the voice from behind her. "The eyes are way too beady." Elspeth turned to find the

Cheese, a large wheel of orange cheddar, aged by design and scarred by battle. Once self-centered and aloof, he had recently become a well-respected officer of the law.

"Rodney!" said Elspeth, wrapping her arms around the Cheese's width—waxy and lumpy from an encounter with the castle's portcullis, the spiked gate meant to serve as a last defense beyond the drawbridge. "Well, if it isn't the Cheese of Police. How are you?"

"Delicious," said the Cheese. "In fact, I've never felt better. You see, the Cheese has been working out. Thirty minutes a day on the treadmill."

Elspeth took a moment to imagine a large wheel of cheese rolling on a treadmill and managed to stifle a laugh. "Well, you certainly do look trimmer," she had to agree. "And younger."

"Oh no," said the Cheese with mock horror. "Never say that to a fine aged cheddar."

"Sorry," said Elspeth. "What I meant is, you don't look the least bit younger. In fact you look downright ancient."

"I bet you say that to all the cheeses," said the Cheese, turning a slightly darker shade of orange.

"Actually, as strange as it might sound, you're the only cheese I know, Rodney," said Elspeth. "Or should I say Officer Cheese?"

"You should say Detective Cheese," said the Cheese.

"You made detective?" gushed Elspeth. "Congratulations."

"Thanks. In fact, the Cheese is on his way to investigate a missing persons case right now. Nobody's seen Peter Peter Pumpkin Eater's wife since Tuesday night."

"Oh," said Elspeth. "Have you tried looking in the pumpkin shell?"

"The pumpkin shell?"

"Yeah. Just an idea. Might be worth a shot."

"Sounds crazy, but I'll check it out," said the Cheese. "Welcome back to the land of the living."

"Thanks," said Elspeth. "It's great to be back."

The Cheese rolled away just as Georgie rushed up, tousled, disheveled, and otherwise looking like a salmon that had just swum upstream. "There you are," he said. "I was afraid the mob had carried you off."

"Gene was just showing me his new statue," said Elspeth.

"Not a bad likeness," Gene said proudly.

"That's a statue of Elspeth and you know it," snapped Georgie. "You are a prop and nothing more."

"Well, well," said Gene. "Sounds like someone's a little jealous. Don't worry. Maybe one day you'll lead an armed rebellion against an evil tyrant and they'll put your picture on a stamp."

"Yes," said Georgie. "Until they find out I made the mistake of saving your pathetic life. Then I'll likely be run out of town."

"When they do," said Gene, "can I have your stuff?"

Sticks and stones may break my bones,
But Gene will ever charm me.

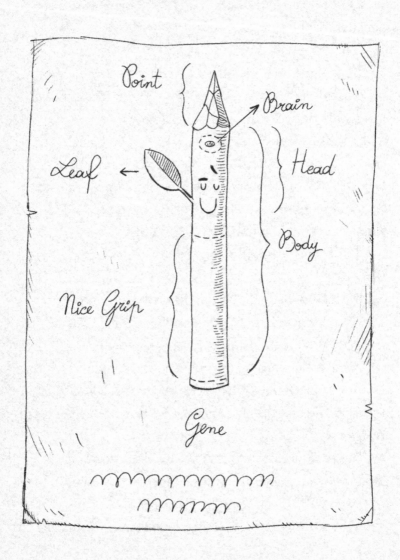

Chapter 5

Georgie led Elspeth and Gene across the courtyard and through the entrance to the Great Hall, which was empty and echoey. This stood in striking contrast to the first time Elspeth had entered that very same room to find it set up for what she had assumed was a magnificent feast in her honor. The feast had indeed been splendid, but, as Elspeth soon discovered, it was meant in no way to honor her but to celebrate her capture and, if Krool had gotten his way, her eventual execution.

That the room was empty now was not surprising. A large hall designed for banquets and other celebrations was of little use at a time like this, when the entire kingdom was in a state of grief.

In just a short time upon the throne, Farrah had become a true queen of the people, simply by taking their concerns seriously. It was because of her tireless efforts that both health care and education were now rights of all citizens of New Winkieland, rather than privileges afforded only to the rich.

She had Krool's private golf course turned into a public park, and she was successful in reinstituting the forty-hour workweek so families would have more time to enjoy it. She refused to be surrounded by bodyguards, protective walls, or anything else that would make her less accessible to her loyal subjects. She granted an audience to anyone who requested it, and the people adored their queen for all she'd done for them. All this made Farrah's safe return all the more important and put even greater pressure on the one to whom they all looked to make this happen.

As Elspeth approached the heavy wooden door at the far end of the hall, she felt suddenly anxious. On the other side of that door was the throne room where Winkie, along with his team of advisors, waited for Elspeth to advise them on what they should do. Each of Winkie's aides secretly hoped her presence would serve as a calming influence on the king, his anxiety having grown more infectious in recent days.

Following strict royal protocol, Elspeth would stand outside the door while Georgie entered the throne room to announce her arrival. He cleared his throat and the room fell instantly silent. Dumpty adjusted his tie, and

Bo-Peep brushed a strand of straw-colored hair away from her face. The three visually impaired mice stood shoulder to shoulder and snapped to attention.

"Your Royal Highness," Georgie bellowed. "I present Lady Elspeth the Conqueror, Duchess of the Deadlands, Countess of Charing Cross, Baroness of . . ."

"Oh, for crying out loud, just let her in, would you?" Winkie snapped.

"Just following protocol, sir," said Georgie defensively, before whispering to Elspeth that she should now enter the room.

Before doing so, she leaned Gene against the wall. "I think it's best if you wait here for now," she whispered.

"Good idea," said Gene. "I wouldn't want to steal your thunder. After all, I do tend to light up a room."

Elspeth smiled at Gene and shook her head, then walked into the room as she felt a person with a statue erected in her honor should: with dignity and aplomb. Though she had been warned of Winkie's deteriorating mental and physical state, she was not fully prepared for just how awful he actually looked. He'd definitely lost weight and maybe even a bit of height, which is particularly problematic for someone so small to begin with.

"Elspeth!" he shouted a little too loudly as he made his way toward her, his eyes glazed and far too mobile in their sockets. "I'm so glad you're here."

Elspeth took a knee, due not so much to the king's status but to his stature. After all, it's really the only way to greet a man no taller than a houseplant.

"King William," she said, trying very hard not to show the full level of concern she felt for him at that moment. "I'm so sorry to hear the horrible news."

"Yes," Winkie sobbed. "It's downright dreadful, isn't it? Look at me. I haven't slept in days. All night long I just lie in bed imagining how awful it must be for her. How frightened and alone she must feel. Oh, whatever shall we do?"

Winkie's chest heaved, and his sobs grew deeper and louder until, without warning, Elspeth reached out and slapped him sharply across the face. The sobs immediately ceased, replaced by gasps throughout the room.

"You . . . you hit me," said Winkie, rubbing his reddened cheek.

"Sorry," said Elspeth. "It's just that we've got a pretty big challenge ahead of us, and I can't have you acting like a blubbering idiot."

"Yes," said Winkie, drying his eyes. "I suppose you're right. I've really got to pull myself together here."

"Don't worry," said Elspeth. "We'll get her back. One way or another." And though her words seemed to calm Winkie somewhat, she did wonder what that one way or another might be. But that's why the king's advisors had gathered in council—to try and figure out the answer to this awful mess.

In addition to Bo-Peep, the king's chief military advisor and leader of the Quick Stick Brigade, the consortium included: Earl Grey, James Brown, and Barry White, who tended to the king's day-to-day business and personal affairs; Fergus, his Minister of Education; and Dumpty, his Minister of Intelligence, dressed in his best tuxedo in honor of Elspeth's arrival.

Bo-Peep was the first to approach Elspeth. "Hello," the woman said in a soft, fluid voice that belied the warrior deep within her. She smiled, but her face looked no less serious as a result. Elspeth wondered if there was a time when she was not quite so earnest. "As always, it's so good to see you."

"It's good to be back," said Elspeth. Casting formalities aside, she stood and hugged her friend. When the two parted, there was Dumpty, waiting his turn.

"Good day there, young lady," he said in that smooth-as-glass British accent that Elspeth could sit and listen to all day.

"I've missed you so much," she said. "I've missed the sound of your voice. Go on, say it for me. Just once. Please?"

"Oh, very well," the half man, half egg replied. As much as it embarrassed him, it had become a ritual now. He cleared his throat briefly. "The name is Dumpty. Humpty Dumpty."

Elspeth showed her appreciation with a broad smile and a solo round of applause. "I love it," she said. "Life in the Deadlands is nothing like it is here. In fact, it's no fun at all."

"Life here isn't much fun lately either, I'm afraid," said Bo-Peep.

"Yes," said Elspeth, suddenly aware that perhaps she had taken too playful a tone with Dumpty considering the situation.

"Let's get down to business, shall we?" said Winkie. "Tell us, Elspeth. We're dying to hear your plan."

"My plan?"

"Yes. For bringing Queen Farrah back to me. After all, that's why I sent for you. I mean, if anyone can solve the problem it's you and your kick-butt attitude."

For the first time Elspeth could see the downside of being a legend in one's own time. People begin to see you as a larger-than-life bronze statue rather than as a person bound by the same laws of nature and physical limitations as everyone else.

"So, what is it then?" asked Winkie. "Tell us. How shall we handle this?"

The look in Winkie's eyes was so full of desperation that Elspeth couldn't bear to tell him that she had absolutely no idea how to approach the situation. So instead, she decided to stall and, if necessary, to lie. "My plan," she said, "is very simple. What we should do is, we should just . . . I mean, it's quite obvious that all we have to do is—"

Just when Elspeth felt as though Winkie might fall over from leaning forward in anticipation, the door to the room swung open and in walked a castle guard, red-faced and short of breath.

"Pardon me, Your Highness," the doughy man panted.

"What is the meaning of this intrusion?" demanded Winkie. He approached the guard with chest out and hands attached firmly to his hips.

"I bring word from the dungeon, Your Majesty."

"You interrupted a meeting pertaining to the safe return of the queen in order to bring me word from the dungeon? Let me guess. The prisoners are complaining about the food again."

"No, My Lord. I mean, yes. But there's more. It's Krool."

"Krool is complaining about the food?"

"No, sir. He claims to have a remedy for the kidnapping situation."

"That's ridiculous," said Winkie. "How could one confined to a prison cell possibly be of any value to us?"

"I don't know, sir. He said he will discuss it only with Lady Elspeth."

ID # 13759KK6

Name: King Krool
Eyes: Blue
Hair: Black
Heart: Black

Bah, bah, black heart
Have you any shame?
No sir, no sir, I'll explain.
It's fun to be monstrous,
It's fun to cause pain,
It's fun for what little joy
It gives to my brain.

Chapter 6

The last time Elspeth visited the dungeon was when Krool himself had sent her there to await execution for the crimes of treason and sedition. Now she was returning for the first time since being rescued by the three visually impaired mice, and she found the walk down the dank and narrow stone stairway to be unnerving to say the least.

She shuddered when she stopped to think about how close she had come to losing her head as well as her hand, for she had also been convicted of stealing a tart.

The farther down they went, the more claustrophobic and panicked she felt at the idea of seeing the face that had haunted her dreams since she'd last laid eyes upon it.

The guard's ring of keys jangled like chains as he

searched for the one that would open the last of many doors separating the castle's prison population from polite society.

The door swung open with a ghostly groan, and the guard stepped aside to allow Elspeth entry into the under-lit cellblock, a long narrow corridor with stone cubicles on either side, enclosed with black iron bars.

"I'll be right out here should you need me," said the guard. "Last cell on the left. Whatever you do, keep your distance from the bars. You never know to what degree a desperate man might go."

"Don't worry," said Elspeth. "I know exactly what he's capable of."

Whereas once the dungeon had been filled to capacity with those who dared speak out against Krool, most of the two dozen cells sat empty since his reign of terror had ended. These days the castle prison was home to but four convicts in all. One was the Crooked Man, found guilty of treason and espionage for his role in Krool's takeover. He now stood, more crooked than ever, in his gray flannel prison uniform, his crooked fingers clutch-ing the iron bars, his face locked in a crooked sneer.

"You," he snarled as Elspeth walked slowly by. "You'll be sorry. One day I'll be out of here. And when that time comes, you'd better watch your back."

"Oh, blow it out your crooked ear," she said and kept moving.

In the next cell was Tom, Tom the piper's son, serving a nine-month sentence for his incorrigible pig stealing. His lawyer had argued that he should instead be sentenced to rehab for his severe bacon addiction. The ploy had proved unsuccessful, and now the young pork enthusiast took no notice of Elspeth as he sat with his back against one wall while repeatedly throwing a small rubber ball against another.

In a third cell was a small, brown monkey with a long, ratty tail. As Elspeth would later learn, the monkey had been jailed for violating a restraining order taken out against him by the weasel. Apparently, chasing someone around a cobbler's bench until they pop is looked upon as harassment. Elspeth walked past his cell, and the monkey flashed an overly toothy grin and raised his eyebrows twice in succession.

As different as each of these inmates were, they all had one thing in common. All of their crimes paled in comparison to those carried out by the man who sat in the last cell on the left. Among the most egregious of those offenses were treason, unspeakable war crimes, and murder.

A beam of yellow light angled into the cell from a small window above, hitting Krool's uncommonly handsome face at such an angle as to make him look even more wicked than Elspeth had remembered. Other than that, however, for a person who had been locked up for several years, local time, Elspeth thought Krool looked remarkably well put together. His cheeks were full, red, and freshly shaved, and he smelled faintly of cologne. His eyes were bright and his teeth still impossibly straight and white. In fact, he looked virtually no different than he had when Elspeth first met him.

She remembered how charmed she had been by him that day and how well he was able to mask his true intentions, which is exactly what makes a man like Krool so dangerous.

From his position on the cot at the back of the cell, the man who had once tried to do away with Elspeth by throwing her down a well as a baby looked up, moving only his eyes. When he finally spoke, his voice was so raspy and whispery that it almost seemed intentional.

"Good afternoon, Elspeth," said Krool with a smile guaranteed to make small children cry and puppies whimper. "I'm absolutely delighted to see you again. Tell me, have the lambs stopped screaming?"

"Lambs?" Elspeth scrunched up her nose. "What lambs?"

"Why, Little Bo-Peep's sheep, of course, which I ate with some fava beans, mint jelly, and a nice Chianti. You still wake up sometimes, don't you? You wake up in the dark and hear the screaming of the lambs."

"Uh, no. Actually I don't," said Elspeth. "That's never happened. Not even once."

"And you think that if only you'd been able to save Bo-Peep's little lambs you could make them stop, don't you?"

"Listen," said Elspeth flatly. "I have no idea what you're babbling about. All I know is that you told one of the guards that you have some big idea about how to get Queen Farrah back safely, which I sincerely doubt."

"So cynical," said Krool with a click of his tongue and a shake of his head.

"Okay then," said Elspeth, folding her arms across her chest. "Let's hear it."

"It's quite simple," said Krool. He rose from the cot and walked smoothly, almost as if floating, to the bars. He gripped them gently but firmly and pushed his chiseled face through as far as the gap would permit. Elspeth took a step back, casually so as not to show the sudden fear that even the bars between them could not ameliorate. "All you have to do," he said, "is meet her demands."

Elspeth's uneasiness quickly turned to disgust. She scoffed and threw up her hands. "I knew this was a waste of time," she said. She turned and called to the guard outside. "Okay! All finished here."

"Wait," said Krool. "Trust me. You'll want to hear what I have to say."

The guard opened the door and leaned in. Elspeth waved him off, and he ducked back into the hallway.

"You've got five minutes," said Elspeth.

"Ample time to lay out such a simple plan," said Krool. "It's my understanding that Mary Mary is asking for one million sixpence."

"Yes," said Elspeth. "And thanks to you and your personal bowling alley and private go-cart track, and your ridiculous royal yacht, there's nothing left in the treasury."

"Oh, there's plenty left," said Krool, closely examining the fingernails of his right hand, which seemed terribly well-manicured considering his whereabouts. "Plenty of money for a person who's willing to look for it."

"What are you talking about?"

Krool's grin became more sinister yet, and he turned his gaze from his fingernails back to Elspeth. "Deep down, whether he'd care to admit it or not, every despot knows his days are numbered," he said. "It's just the nature of the business. Those who overthrow will one day themselves be overthrown. The wise among us prepare for it by putting a little something away for a rainy day should we ever find ourselves living in exile."

"You're saying you still have some of the money you stole from the royal coffers?"

"Stole?" Krool seemed genuinely offended. "I prefer to think of it as an investment in my future."

Elspeth's narrowing eyes showed her skepticism. "How much?"

"Two million sixpence and change, in the form of twenty thousand one-hundred-sixpence notes."

"Twenty thousand one-hundred-sixpence notes?" Elspeth snarled. "Haven't you people heard of the metric system?"

Krool ignored the question, as such things were of no concern to him. "That's one million sixpence for me," he said. "And one million for you and your precious Farrah. Anything left after that? Hey, buy yourself something nice."

"I don't get it," said Elspeth. "What interest could you possibly have in money when you're serving a life sentence? I mean, you could have fourteen million elevenpence and it wouldn't do you any good."

"Not possible," said Krool. "The elevenpence note was taken out of circulation decades ago. As far as my plans for the money, that brings us to part two of my fantastic solution." He turned and walked back to his cot, sat down, then stretched out on his back as if he were about to take a nap. "In exchange for my staggering generosity, Winkie will grant me a full pardon."

Elspeth couldn't decide whether she disliked Krool more for his evil nature or his unrivaled arrogance. "But you killed Fergus's wife. And Bo-Peep's sheep. And you traumatized Little Miss Muffet. And had Little Jack Horner's thumbs broken over a Christmas pie. You've committed so many crimes I can't even name them all."

"Then perhaps you should do as I do," said Krool, "and simply refer to them as my greatest hits."

"It's not funny," said Elspeth. "These are serious

crimes. And now you want King William to drop all charges against you? And let you go?"

"Once he does, I will take you directly to the money." Krool clasped his fingers together and rested his hands upon his chest. "After that, you'll go off to save your little queen, and I will slip away to live out my halcyon days on a tropical island."

"You're crazy," said Elspeth. "King William will never go for that."

"Then he'd best get used to the idea of being wed to a muskrat, hadn't he?" said Krool. "After all, it's not as though you have a better idea, is it?"

Elspeth glowered at the former ruler. "I'm working on it," she said.

"I'm sure you are," said Krool. "By the way, congratulations on your statue. Do you know where they got the bronze for it?"

"No idea."

"By melting down the statue of me that once stood where yours does now," said Krool. "Tell me, Elspeth my dear. How long after you fail to rescue the queen—how long after she's turned into a muskrat—do you think it'll be before they tear down that statue of yours and return it to the smelting pot?"

"I don't care about that stupid statue," Elspeth insisted.

She tried to convince herself that she had no

emotional attachment to it. The statue was merely a symbol, albeit one of the love and admiration bestowed upon her by an adoring public. But this was not about a statue. It was about the fear of disappointing those who had taken so much stock in her. And, more important, it was about the safe return of Queen Farrah. If she failed, the humiliation of having the statue torn down would be nothing compared to the pain of losing her friend.

"How do I know you're not lying?" she asked. "About the money?"

Krool chuckled lightly and sat up again. "Just look at me," he said. "I've been locked up here for nearly two years. You'll have to agree I'm looking awfully fit, considering. At least compared to those poor saps in the other cells. While they dine on watered-down gruel, I subsist on smoked meats, expensive wines, and fine cheeses."

Krool leaned forward and reached beneath his cot. When he straightened up again he was holding what appeared to be a lumpy pillowcase. From inside the pillowcase, he pulled out a wedge of soft white cheese wrapped in brown paper. "You probably thought that pungent odor you smelled was that awful monkey in the cage next door."

Elspeth looked over to find the monkey sticking his head between the bars, still staring at her with that impossibly toothy grin.

"Actually, he does smell pretty bad," said Elspeth.

"Yes," Krool agreed. "Luckily I've got this to help cover up the stench. Epoisses de Bourgogne. Would you care for a bite?"

"I'm good," Elspeth replied. "Where did you get that?"

"You can come by virtually anything in prison, providing you have the ability to pay for it," said Krool. He pinched off a portion of the imported French cheese and popped it between his perfectly shaped lips. "Make no mistake, the money is every bit as real as the stench of that monkey. And it's just sitting there waiting to be put to good use. So, what do you say?"

"It's not up to me," said Elspeth. "All I can do is bring your proposal to the king. After that, it's out of my hands."

"Very well," said Krool as he reached into the pillowcase once more and pulled out a bottle of Chablis. "Just remember, when you do rescue the queen, and you're looking for just the right wine for the celebration, I know a guy."

"I'm twelve," said Elspeth as she turned to leave. "But thanks anyway."

"Oh, one more thing," added Krool.

Elspeth stopped and turned back toward the cell. "Yes?"

"When Winkie agrees to my terms—and he will agree to them—I want it all in writing."

One, two, three, four, five,
Once I caught old Krool alive.
Six, seven, eight, nine, ten,
Then I let him go again.
Why did you let him go?
Because he still has all the dough.

Chapter 7

Elspeth was pretty sure that Krool's terms, whether in writing or not, would be a tough sell with Winkie. And when she returned to the throne room to inform Winkie of the demands, she discovered she was absolutely right.

"A pardon?" King William sneered as he paced angrily about. His advisors made sure to give plenty of room to his flailing arms and stomping feet. "He's crazy if he thinks I'm going to just let him go. After all the pain and suffering he's caused. There's got to be another way."

"Actually, there are two other ways, as I see it," said Elspeth.

A sudden wave of hope washed across Winkie's ashen and unshaven face. "Yes? Well? What are they?"

"The first is to defy Mary Mary and try and get Queen Farrah back without giving her anything."

"No, no, that won't do," said Winkie. "Far too dangerous.

The queen's life is at stake. You don't know what we're dealing with here. Mary Mary is very dangerous and highly unpredictable. So, what's the other way?"

"A bake sale."

"A bake sale?" Winkie snorted. "What kind of ridiculous idea is that?"

Georgie's faced reddened. "I was thinking maybe a raffle too," he mumbled. A look of disdain from everyone in the room caused his eyes to fall to the same floor that Winkie continued to pace until finally the king sighed and fell back onto his tiny throne.

"The point is," said Elspeth, "that as much as we all despise Krool, we really don't have much of a choice but to deal with him."

Winkie placed his cheeks between his palms and appeared to be trying to pull his own face off. "Dealing with him is one thing. But letting him go? How could I, in good conscience, issue a pardon to the man who murdered Bo-Peep's sheep? And Fergus's lovely wife?"

"Don't worry about it," said Fergus. "If there's anyone who would love to see Krool rot in jail until the end of time, it's me. But the fact is that nothing will bring my Vera back."

"Yes," Bo-Peep agreed. "The important thing now is not to lose another. We must do whatever it takes to ensure the queen's safe return."

"You are noble friends indeed," said Winkie with a stiff smile. "But it's important to remember that this is Krool we're dealing with here. How do we know all this isn't some kind of a trick? How do we know he really has the money?"

"Whether it amounts to two million sixpence, I can't say for sure," said Elspeth. "But he does have money. Trust me. He may be a lowly prisoner, but he eats like a king. Fine wines, smoked meats, imported cheese. Pretty much whatever he wants."

This news seemed to deeply trouble the actual king, who hadn't eaten in days due to stress and grief. "So he's managed to corrupt someone in my Royal Guard," said Winkie. "This is horrible indeed."

"Perhaps not," said Bo-Peep, with a spark in her eye and a quick twirl of her staff that ended in her palm with a loud smack. "This could be the best news we've had in some time."

"I don't understand," said Winkie. "How could corruption within my inner ranks be anything but awful?"

"Because," said Bo-Peep. "In order to bribe your guards, he has to have access to the money."

"Yes," said Dumpty, his face at once filled with intrigue, his eyes flashing like Bo-Peep's. "Unless the money is hidden somewhere in his cell, which would be quite impossible, he has someone on the outside, bringing him the funds."

"Precisely," said Fergus, the excitement in the room spreading like a brush fire. The owl fluttered from his perch upon the window ledge and landed on the high back of the throne. "Which means there's someone besides Krool who knows where it's hidden."

And so there it was. A sudden and simple solution to the current situation. All they had to do was determine who had remained loyal to Krool and was now supplying him with the money he needed to live in relative comfort while locked away from the world. It was a task easier said than done, given that they had only four days to meet Mary Mary's deadline.

"But where would we start?" asked Winkie, giving voice to what they all were thinking. "We can't interrogate every citizen of Banbury Cross. That could take weeks."

"We should start with the guards," said Elspeth, who had watched a good many detective shows in her young life. "If we can figure out which of them is on the take, maybe we can get him to flip on Krool's supplier."

"It's a long shot," said Dumpty. "And it might slow us down by a day."

"I don't care," said Winkie. He stood up and planted a fist firmly into the palm of his hand. "If we can somehow get the money without pardoning Krool, it's definitely worth the effort."

Elspeth was excited and honored yet nervous. She had never before been asked to be part of a police interrogation. But the Cheese was insistent that a person of her assertiveness would be a valuable addition to the process.

"How shall we do it?" she asked, while frantically pacing the floor of the Banbury Cross police station. "How about the old good cheese, bad cheese routine?"

"I prefer the bad cheese, bad cheese approach," said the Cheese. "Just follow my lead and you'll do fine."

There were only a half dozen guards who performed dungeon duty at any given time, and the first to be summoned to the interrogation room was a long-time employee of the castle by the name of Solomon Grundy.

"Please, sit down, Mr. Grundy," Detective Cheese instructed the tired-looking man, who made no effort to hide his annoyance at having been called away from his supper.

Grundy took a seat at the table, every bit as bare as the room's white walls, except for a pitcher of water and an empty glass. "You mind telling me what this is all about?" he grumbled.

"We'll ask the questions around here," said the Cheese, setting the tone of the interrogation early. "You got that?"

The Cheese rolled slowly around the room while Elspeth leaned back against the edge of the table, trying very hard to look as though she'd done this a million times.

"Sure," said Grundy. "How long is this going to take?"

The Cheese stared flatly at Grundy. "Did you just ask another question?" Grundy responded by looking furtively about the room.

"Tell us now, Mr. Grundy," Elspeth jumped in. "You dungeon guards aren't exactly getting rich keeping an eye on all those dangerous criminals, are you?"

"Ha," Grundy replied. He ran his hand angrily through his thinning hair. "Ever since the union got run out, we can barely put hot cross buns on the table."

"That's what I thought," Elspeth replied. "So then, who could really blame a person in your position for wanting to make a little extra on the side?"

Grundy folded his arms and leaned back in the chair. "What are you talking about?"

"You know darn well what she's talking about," hissed the Cheese. "She's talking about bribes."

"Bribes?" Grundy exploded. "How dare you accuse me of such a thing. I've never taken a bribe in my twenty-two years on the job."

The Cheese scoffed loudly. "Yeah?" he said. "Well, one of you guards has been taking money from Krool in exchange for fine wine and stinky cheese. Now don't get me wrong, some of my best friends are stinky cheeses. But this has to do with more than stinky cheese. In fact, everything about this stinks to high heaven."

"I agree," said Grundy. He leaned forward in the chair

and casually poured himself a glass of water. "But you're wasting your time with me," he said. "Sounds like the guy you want to talk to is Tucker."

"Who's Tucker?" asked Elspeth.

Grundy took a sip of water and wiped his mouth with the back of his hand. "Little Tommy Tucker," he said. "One of the guards. Young guy. Only been on the job a couple of years. Anyway, I ran into him on his day off last weekend. Out by the stream. He was row, row, rowing his brand-new boat gently down it, if you know what I mean."

"Sounds like he's living pretty high on the hog," said a suddenly intrigued Detective Cheese.

"Oh yeah," said Grundy. "Let's just say he doesn't exactly have to sing for his supper these days. And there's more. Lots more."

"We're listening," said Elspeth.

Moments later, just outside the room, the office secretary, a prim woman named Polly, sat at her very tidy desk, typing up a report on the case of Mrs. Pumpkin Eater, which had been solved that afternoon when she was found quite unharmed in a hollowed-out gourd. Polly stopped typing when the door to the interrogation room opened and out walked Grundy, followed closely by Elspeth and Detective Cheese.

"You're free to go for now," said Elspeth. "But don't leave town."

"That's right," echoed the Cheese. "And so help me, if I find out you're not being straight with the Cheese, I'll throw the book at you faster than you can say *if Peter Piper picked a peck of pickled peppers, how many pickled peppers did Peter Piper pick?* You got that?"

"I think so," said Grundy, who had never been very good at tongue twisters. Elspeth and the Cheese watched as the tired and hungry guard loped off toward the exit. Then the Cheese turned to his secretary.

"Hey, Polly," he said. "I need you to find Dumpty for me. Tell him we need to speak to a guard by the name of Tommy Tucker right away."

"Will do," said Polly, pushing back from her desk.

"Oh, and Polly?" said the Cheese.

"Yes?"

"Put the kettle on. It's gonna be a long night."

Little Tommy Tucker sold Krool some supper,
Fine stinky cheese and fresh bread and butter.
Will he row merrily right down the stream?
Or be sent up the river for his part in the scheme?

Chapter 8

When Tommy Tucker arrived at the station, he was, unlike Grundy, overly congenial and visibly nervous. He was escorted by an officer in uniform to the interrogation room, where he sat alone for a time, fidgeting and drumming his fingers on the table with enough force to create ripples in the water pitcher.

Outside the room, through a window of one-way glass, Elspeth and Detective Cheese observed the suspect, paying close attention to the man's body language.

"Well? What do you think?" asked the Cheese. "What's your gut telling you?"

"Sure looks guilty to me," Elspeth replied.

They watched as Tucker sighed and rubbed the back of his neck then filled the water glass. His shaky hands betrayed him—leaving a glass half full and a small puddle on the table. He was mopping up the water with the sleeve of his shirt when the door opened and in rolled the Cheese, closely followed by Elspeth.

"Evening, Mr. Tucker," said the Cheese. "Appreciate you coming in on such short notice."

"No problem," said Tucker with a tight smile, hiding his wet sleeve beneath the table. "Always happy to help out law enforcement."

"Glad to hear that," said the Cheese. "Because I need you to help me understand something, Tommy. You mind if I call you Tommy?"

"Not at all," said Tucker.

"Great," said the Cheese. "Let me ask you something, Tommy. Heard you got yourself a brand-new boat recently."

Tommy's face dropped as he instantly realized why he had been summoned to the station. "Yes," he admitted. "Just a row boat. Nothing fancy."

"Where'd you get the money for it?" Elspeth demanded.

"Well, I . . . I saved up," Tucker sputtered. He took a quick drink of the water and choked on it a little.

The Cheese scoffed and spat on the floor. "Saved up? Ha! Give me a break. You're dirty, Tommy. You're in Krool's back pocket, and you know it."

"That's a lie!" Tucker protested in a way that Elspeth thought was a bit too adamant. "I don't know what you're talking about." With his dry shirtsleeve he wiped away a pool of sweat that had gathered on his upper lip.

"You know, I spoke to a couple of your neighbors, Tommy boy," said the Cheese. "According to them, just yesterday you went to market to buy a fat hog, then came home again looking all jiggety-jog."

"I . . . I can explain that," Tucker stammered. "I won that hog. In a contest."

"Oh really?" said Elspeth. "What kind of contest?"

"Uh . . . hog-calling contest?"

The Cheese rolled behind Tucker and leaned very close to the man's ear. "You and I have a little problem here, Tommy. Because I'm not picking up what you're throwing down." The Cheese's voice was just above a whisper now. "I got witnesses who saw you at the casino last weekend playing knick-knack paddywhack. They said you dropped a cool ten thousand sixpence in twenty minutes then threw the dog a bone like you were made of bones."

"That was just money I won earlier. I swear it. I was up big at the blackjack table."

"You sure are a lucky man, aren't you?" said Elspeth. "Winning a hog-calling contest. Cleaning up at the casino. It sounds almost too good to be true."

"Well, what can I tell you?" Tucker chuckled awkwardly.

"You can start by telling us what we wanna hear." The Cheese had suddenly abandoned his whisper in favor of a booming baritone that ricocheted off the empty walls. "You listen to me and you listen good, Tommy. We're giving you one chance to come clean. One chance to cut a deal for a lesser sentence."

Tucker's eyes darted about the stark white room until he caught his reflection in the one-way glass. He was surprised at how guilty he looked. "But I haven't done anything," he insisted.

"Okay," said the Cheese, rolling back around to face Tucker. "Have it your way. But make no mistake. Once you leave this room, the offer is off the table. And then I'm gonna be all over you like cheese on a cracker. Now, you sure there's not something you wanna tell us, Tommy?"

Tucker's breathing became increasingly shallow, his eyes ever more shifty. A bead of sweat meandered down his forehead, followed by another. And then, finally, he broke. "Okay," Tucker sobbed. "I'll tell you what you want to know. But please, I can't go to prison. I've got a family."

"I can't promise you won't do some time in the joint," said the Cheese. "But I give you my word that I'll ask the judge to go easy on you. Now, tell us everything."

Outside the room, Dumpty, who had just arrived at the station, watched through the one-way glass as Tucker blubbered into his hands while telling Elspeth and the Cheese all that he knew. That the confession lasted only ten minutes indicated that he didn't know a lot. But it was more than enough.

The door to the room opened, and out came Elspeth and the Cheese to find Dumpty waiting for them.

"Well?" said Dumpty, his eyes transfixed on Tommy, who was now pacing the room in a state of anguish.

"We grilled him like a grilled cheese sandwich," said Elspeth with a smile.

"And?"

"He cracked like an egg."

"That's right," said the Cheese. "Gave up everything. Says our guy is a dude who goes by the name of the Muffin Man."

"The Muffin Man?" gasped Dumpty. "Who lives on Drury Lane?"

"No. Different Muffin Man. This guy works the Lower East Side. Fifty-Fourth and Mulberry. First name Larry."

"Nice work," said Dumpty, with a smile of pure relief and giddy anticipation at the thought of telling Krool just what he could do with his offer. "Nice work indeed."

"Thanks," said Elspeth.

A long night of interrogation had taken a physical and emotional toll, and the Cheese rolled over to the office break station for much needed refreshment. "Can I offer you a cup of tea, Elspeth?"

"Sure," she replied.

"Dumpty?"

"Delighted."

Suddenly, the Cheese frowned and exhaled in disgust.

He turned to his secretary, who was reading a message that had just been delivered. "Hey, Polly. I thought I told you to put the kettle on."

"I did," said Polly. "But Sukey took it off again."

The Cheese fumed and turned a darker shade of orange. "You tell Sukey to keep her hands off my tea kettle. Now get a message to dispatch. Tell 'em I need a couple of plainclothes guys to pick up Larry the Muffin Man and bring him downtown right away."

"I'm afraid that won't be possible," said Polly.

"What do you mean that won't be possible? Why not?"

"This just came in," said Polly. She leaned over her desk and handed the message to Elspeth.

"Well, what is it?" asked the Cheese.

"According to this," said Elspeth, "the Muffin Man's wife found him dead earlier this evening. Floating face-down in a vat of muffin batter."

Dumpty and the Cheese stood in stunned silence, the air instantly taken out of their sails.

"Well, ain't that a pocket full of posies," said the Cheese finally. "I can tell you one thing. This was no accident. And it ain't no coincidence."

"Krool," Elspeth agreed. "I guess he's got more friends than we thought."

"B-i-n-g-o," said the Cheese. "Bingo."

Suddenly none of them felt too much like a celebratory cup of tea. Since Krool's reign had come to an end, violent crimes were rare in Banbury Cross. In fact, this was the first murder since the killing of Cock Robin, a crime that, two years later, remained unsolved.

And though the Muffin Man may have contributed to his own murder by involving himself with the likes of Krool, the news of his death was unnerving and depressing all the same. And whether or not Krool had a hand in the Muffin Man drowning in a battery grave, one thing was certain. They were once again playing by Krool's rules.

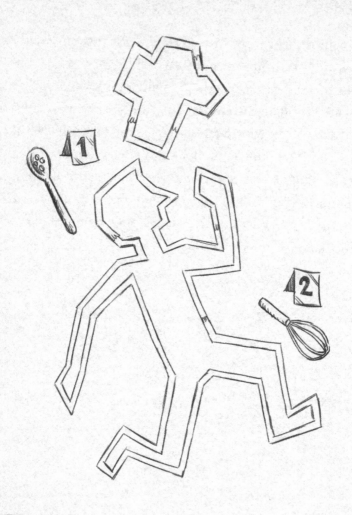

Did you know the Muffin Man, the Muffin Man, the
   Muffin Man?
Did you know the Muffin Man, Larry was his name?
Yes, I knew the Muffin Man, the Muffin Man, the Muffin Man
Yes, I knew the Muffin Man, but now I fear he's slain.

Chapter 9

Winkie's advisors had been summoned to the throne room once more, both to offer support and to witness the transaction that was taking place.

"May I remind Your Majesty that this is a legally binding agreement," said Jeremy Nod of Wynken, Blynken, and Nod, the best law firm in Banbury Cross.

"You don't have to remind me," said Winkie.

Nod, with his well-manicured fingers, slid the small stack of papers across the tiny table where Winkie sat, his face red from rage and high blood pressure, his own fingertips white from squeezing the pen much harder than it was designed to be squeezed.

"Just sign right there," said Nod.

Winkie looked at each and every face in the room before expelling one last angry sigh then scrawled his name above the line at the bottom of the page.

"And initial here," Nod added, flipping to a new page. "And here."

Winkie scratched out a quick triple *W* on the indicated spaces then sat back, closed his eyes, and pinched the bridge of his nose. "When I had discovered that my lovely Farrah was missing," he said, "and when the ransom note arrived, I swore I would make a deal with the devil if necessary in order to get her back. True to my word, that's exactly what I've done."

The king looked at Fergus and Bo-Peep as if he had just stabbed his longtime friends and trusted advisors in the back. "I'm so sorry," he said, lowering his gaze to the table, unable to look them in the eye.

"You did what you had to do," said Bo-Peep. "And each of us would have done the same."

"It's true," said Fergus, placing a sympathetic wing upon Winkie's back. "Sometimes the pill that cures is the most difficult to swallow."

Nod took the document, jogged the pages, and slid them into a large brown envelope then tucked it beneath the arm of his designer suit. "I will witness Krool's signature and return a fully executed copy to Your Highness posthaste," he said.

"Very well," said Winkie, in the way someone would who had just chosen the lesser of two incredible evils. Nod hurried out of the room, and Winkie pushed back from the table and stood. "Well, we'd all better get some rest," he said. "First thing tomorrow, we set out to find the hidden money. That will give us a full three days to travel to the Thick to rescue my sweet Farrah."

Normally when she was a guest of the castle, Elspeth slept soundly and peacefully between the finest linen upon the softest, most inviting mattress. This night would be different. Dark, gruesome dreams woke her several times, each nightmare playing in her head more vividly than the one before. She dreamed of Krool, Mary Mary, and the Great Spiny Gleekin, a creature Elspeth had never seen, though her subconscious did a fine job of creating a very vivid picture.

If that weren't enough, there were the lambs. Though Elspeth would never admit it to Krool and give him the satisfaction of being right, he somehow had been able to describe her nightmares with astonishing accuracy. She did frequently dream about those poor lambs and their horrible fate. How Krool could possibly know such a thing made her wonder if perhaps he had the power to enter her very thoughts.

When she gathered with the others in the throne room early the next morning, it was evident that she was not the only one who had endured a restless night. If the eyes are the windows to the soul, thought Elspeth, you can also tell a lot about a person by looking at the drapes.

Dumpty's eyelids drooped heavily while Bo-Peep's featured puffy bags. Fergus's were completely closed, and Winkie's, by now, were twitching involuntarily and practically nonstop.

In addition to worrying about Farrah and suffering the pangs of buyer's remorse for the deal he'd made with Krool, Winkie had spent much of the night lying awake, trying to decide just who should accompany him on this life-or-death operation. The group, he decided, should be small and unintimidating but capable, each member bringing to the effort a unique or necessary skill.

As the king's chancellor and the person most responsible for his well-being, Georgie was vehemently opposed to this idea. "It's far too dangerous," he said. "We're dealing with an adversary of unknown capabilities. We should be sending our entire army."

"And what do you suppose Mary Mary would think if we marched into the Thick with full forces?" said Winkie. "She'll think we're there to take the queen back by force. We must exude a spirit of cooperation. Besides, there's a chance that this entire thing might be a trick to lure my army from the castle in order to carry out an attack."

It would have to be a small group, Winkie insisted. Those officially tapped to accompany him on the mission were Dumpty, Bo-Peep, and Elspeth, who tensed at the mention of her name. After all, she had promised her father that she was here only for the purpose of consultation and would be going nowhere near the Thick. She felt as though she should speak up, that she should honor

Jack's wishes and insist on remaining behind. But how could she? After all, she was a local hero. And heroes do not disappoint. So instead of objecting, she simply pushed the promise she'd made to Jack from her mind and said nothing.

Winkie also decided that his most trusted guards, Cory, Rory, and Maury, three beefy brothers who had grown up in a shoe, would come along to provide the muscle should it be needed. And they had plenty to spare. Ardent weight lifters, their bodies had become so enormous that their shaved heads looked disproportionately small. Their arms pulsed with veins the size of a towrope, and their washboard abdominals were so defined that the boys could actually use them to do their laundry, their belly buttons acting as a built-in lint trap. Nature thinks of everything.

In addition to King William's hand-picked roster, Elspeth would add another. Despite his penchant for being insufferably annoying, she insisted that she be permitted to bring Gene along for self-defense.

"And don't forget good luck," Gene added. "I'm loaded with it."

Once again Georgie was less than enthusiastic about this arrangement. A stick chosen for this all-important mission while the king's chancellor was ordered to stay behind? Insulting to say the least and, in Georgie's mind, highly imprudent.

"But, Your Highness," he said. "I insist that, as your chancellor and official media spokesperson, I be allowed to join you. It's my sworn duty to tend to your needs."

"What I need most at this time," said Winkie, "is for someone to stay behind and take care of the matters of the castle and of the people of Banbury Cross."

"Very well," said Georgie. He tried not to answer too quickly or sound too eager to agree, as it might appear that he really had no desire at all to go along, being that he was a notorious coward and the idea of dealing with the likes of Mary Mary and her army of monsters made him weak in the knees.

And so the official roster was set.

Of course there was one more who would be part of the group for the first part of the mission. That person was, at that very moment, being made to kneel at the far end of his cell, facing away from the door, with his hands clasped behind his head.

"This is entirely unnecessary," Krool insisted as Maury stood at the door and Rory and Cory each took one of Krool's hands and shackled them together behind his back. "And terribly impolite, I might add. I don't remember seeing anything in the written agreement about being handcuffed."

"That's enough out of you," said Cory, the eldest of the brothers.

That Krool had been responsible for their childhood home being razed, forcing them to grow up living in a large shoe, might have had something to do with the brothers' rough handling of the man who, until he fulfilled his part of the agreement by leading them to the ill-gotten money, would remain a prisoner of the Crown. They pulled Krool to his feet and turned him toward the door.

"Let's go," said Rory, with a sharp nudge to Krool's upper back, a move for which Krool showed his lack of appreciation with a slow turn of his head and a searing glare.

"Really," he said. "There's no need for that, son."

Though Krool's hands were securely bound and in spite of the fact that he was no match for the three brothers physically speaking, the sound of his voice nonetheless would have managed to raise the hair on the backs of their respective necks if those necks hadn't been shaved clean.

"Go on," said Cory, swallowing the lump in his throat that he hoped Krool hadn't noticed. "Get moving."

"Is this any way to treat your former king?" said Krool, asking a question for which he neither expected nor received an answer.

Down the dim corridor the brothers escorted their prisoner, who was practically giddy in anticipation of feeling the sun on his pallid, devilish face for the first time in years. "It's the little things you miss when you're in prison," he said to the highly disinterested brothers. "A walk along the beach in the moonlight, for instance.

Kicking a small child or a puppy. You know, the simple pleasures in life."

They passed through the final door, which took them to the castle courtyard and into the early morning shadow of Elspeth's statue, where Winkie and his team had already assembled.

Krool winced in the natural light and, once his eyes had adjusted to it, he surveyed the group with a squinty smile.

"Well, how nice of you all to be here for my coming-out party," he said. "You all look just as I remember you. Haven't changed a bit. Well, you, Elspeth my dear, look exhausted. Tell me, did the screaming of the lambs keep you up again?"

"I have no idea what you're talking about," said Elspeth, shooting Krool the dirtiest look she could muster.

"Come on. You know," said Krool with one eye trained on Bo-Peep. "A baa-baa here. A baa-baa there. Here a baa. There a baa. Everywhere a baa-baa."

"That's enough out of you, sir," said Dumpty, stepping closer to Krool while fighting the urge to slap the prisoner across his smug, handsome face. And though it would be a gesture aimed at defending Bo-Peep's honor, the woman herself was a master in the art of Shaolin stick fighting and certainly needed no one to act on her behalf.

"Oh, how brave of you," said Krool. "Threatening a man whose hands are tied behind his back."

"Then perhaps we should untie them and settle a few things right here and now," said Dumpty, reflexively clenching his fists.

"Please, it's okay," said Bo-Peep with a quick twirl of her staff. "He'll get his one of these days."

"I'll get mine, all right." Krool smiled. "To the tune of one million sixpence. I'll be sure to send you all a nice postcard from the southern isles. Now, shall we get going?"

Winkie did not like to admit seeing eye to eye with Krool on anything, but he had to agree that, considering Mary Mary's looming deadline, they had better make haste. He clapped twice in quick succession. The stable door across the courtyard opened and eight stablemen led eight horses to where the nine travelers stood. Each would have his own horse while Gene would ride with Elspeth.

Despite the fact that his vertigo troubled him no more, Dumpty, with his oval body and disproportionately small legs and arms, still required a great deal of help from the stablemen to get onto the horse's back.

"Whoa! Easy, lads," he said as he wobbled several times before finally settling into the saddle.

The only other one to have any trouble was the prisoner with his hands shackled behind his back. When the stablemen hoisted Krool up onto the mount, they overshot their mark and the rider nearly fell off the other side.

"This is ridiculous," said Krool. "And barbaric. You can't expect me to ride cross-country with my hands bound like this."

"If you think we're stupid enough to unlock those cuffs, you've got another thing coming," said Gene.

"Suppose I fall off and break my neck?" said Krool. "Then what?"

"Then a parade to celebrate the occasion, I would imagine," said Bo-Peep.

Krool displayed a rigid smile. "Yes, I'm sure there are those who would relish something *baaaaad* happening to me," he said with a chuckle. "The problem is that without me, there's no money. And with no money, there's no Farrah. And with no Farrah, poor King William will have to find another little dolly to play with."

Krool turned to find Winkie, sitting atop his horse, glaring right back. "How dare you speak of the queen in such a manner," he said.

"The truth is often unpleasant," replied Krool. "Doesn't make it any less true. Now, be a good little king and tell your boys to remove these ridiculous shackles."

Winkie seethed in silence, his hatred for Krool and his love for Farrah battling ferociously within the pit of his stomach. As much as he despised Krool, the rancor could not match the affection he felt for his wife. He nodded to Cory. "Remove the cuffs. But if he tries to escape, kill him."

As Cory executed the command, Elspeth could feel Gene bristling beneath her grip. "Come on," he whispered. "Just let me give him one good smack to the back of the head."

"I thought you were a pacifist," Elspeth whispered back.

"Oh, right," said Gene. "How about if *you* smack him on the head? With a stick. A stick like me, for instance."

When all were in position upon their mounts, Winkie looked to Krool once more. "Well?" he said. "Which way to the money?"

"South," said Krool. "In the direction of St. Ives. I'll provide further instructions once we get a little closer. And don't worry. I have no intention of attempting an escape. Say what you will about me, but I am a man of my word. I do what I say I will do. And don't ever forget that."

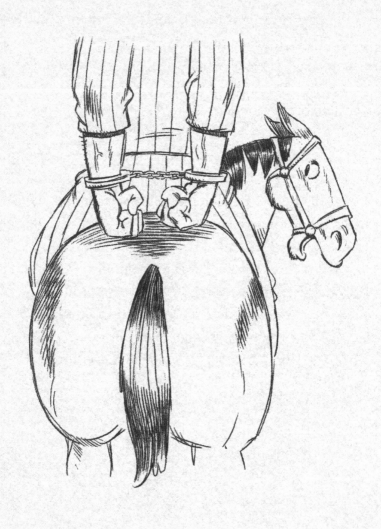

Needles and pins, needles and pins,
When Krool's involved, the trouble begins.

Chapter 10

The drawbridge came down, and the horses, four pairs, side by side, carried their riders across the plank and into the town square where a crowd was gathering in response to a circulating rumor that Krool had been released from prison. The thought of such a thing was so confounding and so unthinkable that it had to be seen to be believed.

The villagers rushed from the cottages and the shops that stood outside the castle walls. They gasped, booed, and hissed upon seeing Krool's self-satisfied and well-fed face. Cory, Rory, and Maury's mother, known as the Old Woman who lived in a shoe, threw a normal-size shoe at that very face, and Krool ducked just in time to avoid it. The shoe continued on and, instead, found the side of Dumpty's head.

"Pardon me, madam," said the indignant egg.

"Sorry," the woman called out.

Little Jack Horner gave Krool a long, loud raspberry and a double thumbs-down with thumbs that had been badly mangled by Krool's henchmen.

It wasn't long before the murmuring and grumbling turned to shouts of anger.

"What in migration is going on here?" cried Goosey Goosey Gander, a goose with a nervous tic and a serious flatulence problem, attributed to eating too many bread-crumbs at the park. "You can't let him go. He's evil. *Honk!* Sorry. Pardon me."

"He's a monster," screamed Little Miss Muffet so loudly that she burped up a small bit of whey.

"He's a murderer," hollered Young Mother Hubbard, whose own mother was one of the many who was alleged to have died at Krool's hands.

Elspeth soon became aware that Jack and Jill were among the crowd when they managed to push their way to the front.

"Elspeth, dear," said Jill, walking alongside Elspeth's horse. "You're not going to the Thick?"

"Don't worry, I'll be fine," she answered.

"You promised you were here only to advise," said Jack.

"I'm sorry," said Elspeth. "But King William asked me to go, and I couldn't let him down in his time of need. You understand."

"I don't understand," said Jack. "And I don't see why they've had to let Krool out of prison."

"I know it's horrible," admitted Elspeth. "But it was the only way."

"But he took you from us," said Jack. He limped along behind his wife on that bad foot, the result of an encounter with a lava-filled sinkhole in Torcano Alley. "And he threw you down a well. And now they're just going to let him go?"

"Proof that our justice system does work," said Krool with a slimy smile, though his eyes remained forward as if the lowly peasants were unworthy of his gaze.

"Why, you," said Jack with his teeth and fists equally clenched. "I ought to pull you down from there and show you a thing or two about how things work."

It was immediately evident that there were plenty among the group who felt it would be an excellent idea to pull Krool from his mount and deliver a dose of vigilante justice, an act that would place the queen's life at serious risk.

"Pardon me, Your Majesty," Dumpty shouted over the rumble. "But don't you think it might be a good idea to address their concerns?"

"I suppose you're right," the king agreed.

He ordered the procession stopped, and he stood upon his horse's saddle, a move that would have had more impact were he not the size of a garden gnome.

"Listen, everyone," the pint-size king spoke with arms outstretched. "May I have your attention please?"

Despite their respect for and allegiance to their king, the people seemed to have collectively decided that, no, he could not have their attention. They continued to express their anger by tossing insults and the odd shoe in Krool's direction while Winkie pleaded for order.

"I demand order," Winkie shouted to little effect.

"You're being too polite," said Gene. "Allow me. Quiet, peasants!"

It wasn't exactly a hush that fell over the crowd, but the sudden reduction in noise was certainly an improvement. It was now almost quiet enough that Winkie could be heard.

"King William has something important to say," Gene continued. "So listen up or get smacked in the back of the head! Got it? Good."

"Thank you, noble stick," said Winkie.

"The name is Gene, remember? There's a statue of me in the courtyard."

"Right, of course," Winkie said with no sign of recognition. He turned his focus back to the unruly masses. "Okay, now listen. I know everyone is quite upset to learn that we've been forced to make certain concessions, as it were, regarding one of our prisoners."

"He's not just any prisoner," shouted Simple Simon. "He's a barbarian."

"He killed my mother," said Young Mother Hubbard.

"He broke my thumbs," yelled Jack Horner.

"He tipped me over and poured me out," cried a teapot named Veronica.

"Yes, yes," Winkie agreed, trying desperately to talk above the grousing that crescendoed with each passing second. "I am well aware of the countless crimes this man has committed. And I know how much you despise him and his mother for having given birth to such a wicked, cowardly, slimy, worthless, lowdown—"

"Okay, I think you've sold it well enough," said Krool, rolling his eyes.

"Filthy, evil degenerate," Winkie finished. "But the fact of the matter is that this evil degenerate has access to money. Money that he siphoned from the royal treasury and hid away. As difficult as it may be to come to terms with, we have no choice but to use that money to pay Mary Mary the ransom she's demanded and bring Queen Farrah back safe and sound."

If Winkie thought this would be enough to bring order he was sadly mistaken, for all it managed to do was strike a nerve of a different sort among the peasant class.

"So that's it," said Simple Simon. "The rich always find a way to beat the system. Same old thing."

This resulted in a very vocal show of agreement that soon drowned out the king's attempts at appeasement.

"I say we *should* let him go," said Little Boy Blue. "Right after we draw and quarter him!"

The mob cheered and surged toward Krool, a move

that spooked the horses. Bo-Peep's reared up on its hind legs and, were she not an expert equestrian, would have thrown her to the ground.

Rory, Cory, and Maury moved their horses in position to form a protective wall around the man who had all but ruined their childhood. And though secretly they would have enjoyed nothing more than to see Krool torn limb from limb, they knew the importance of keeping him alive. For now. Once they got the money, that would be a different story.

"Quiet!" Gene shouted, once more bringing temporary order to the situation.

"Thank you, helpful stick," said Winkie.

"Again, the name is Gene."

"Yes, of course," Winkie replied dismissively. "Now look. I want everyone to know that the Crown does not look lightly upon the serious offenses committed by this prisoner. Indeed we have all suffered at his hands, either directly or indirectly, and I would be happy to see him drawn and quartered. But we can't do that, because if we do the only other way to get the ransom money would be with a bake sale capable of raising one million sixpence in the next three days. Which is an especially unlikely occurrence now that the Muffin Man is dead."

"The Muffin Man?" gasped Goosey Goosey Gander. "Who lived on Drury Lane?"

"He still lives on Drury Lane," said Winkie.

"But you said he was dead," griped the goose. "Make up your mind. *Honk!* Sorry. Pardon me."

"He is dead," said Winkie, quickly losing patience. "I'm talking about the other Muffin Man. Larry, I believe, was his name."

Apparently this muffin man was the far less popular of the two because this bit of information resulted in a collective shrug of indifference from all but Gene. "Great," the easily offended stick sneered. "You remember the name of some random cupcake maker but not the guy who no-handedly restored you to the throne. Nice. Real nice."

"Give it a rest, Gene," said Elspeth sternly.

"So you see what we're up against here," said Winkie. "We have no choice but to let Krool go. But as part of the deal, he has agreed to never set foot in Banbury Cross again."

"And what if he does?" shouted Simple Simon.

"Then you can draw and quarter him," said Winkie.

This seemed to provide enough assurance to the protesters. They finally stepped aside and allowed the procession to continue.

As the horses clopped onward, leaving distance between the travelers and the townspeople, Jack called out, "Don't take your eyes off him, Elspeth. Remember. He's tried twice now to kill you."

And though Elspeth turned and offered Jack and Jill a reassuring nod, she was secretly quite unnerved by the entire situation. And the closer they got to the edge of town and to the wide-open countryside, the more Elspeth feared that at any moment they might fall victim to an ambush. By whom, she didn't know. But apparently the others shared her concern, because as they passed through the city wall the traveling party was tense, hushed, and on high alert. Even Gene seemed to have nothing he deemed worth saying.

After all, the murder of Larry the Muffin Man seemed to be proof positive that Krool still had friends as well as enemies on the outside. But what Elspeth and the others did not realize as they made their way toward St. Ives, was that at that very moment, Detective Cheese was paying a little visit to the Lower East Side of Banbury Cross, also known as the Baking District, to interview witnesses to that murder. And what those witnesses saw would turn out to be nothing short of astounding.

The itsy bitsy rider stood up to hush the crowd.
The crowd went insane and drowned the rider out.
Out came the stick and called for some restraint.
And the itsy bitsy rider addressed the crowd again.

Chapter
11

With Elspeth well on her way to pick up Krool's stolen loot, the Cheese would have to continue his investigation without her help. He rolled along the cracked and garbage-strewn sidewalks cast in shadow from the old brick buildings, well covered with graffiti, some of it obscene, some of it nonsensical, all of it perfectly rhymed.

He spun his way past a shop painted with the words, "They're all going to St. Ives, with a man who's ruined lives."

The Baking District, famous for its mouth-watering pies, tarts, and hot cross buns, was also quite well known for something far less savory. It had become, in recent years, a hotbed of crime and black-market trading. It was said you could find anything you were looking for in the

Baking District, so long as you had enough money and a certain lack of regard for your physical safety. And Detective Cheese was looking for answers.

He rolled past Larry the Muffin Man's place, still cordoned off with yellow police tape as his forensics team continued to search for fingerprints, hair samples, and anything else that might help solve the case.

Next door to the muffin shop was another bakery, this one specializing in cakes, pies, and donuts. Detective Cheese entered through the open door unnoticed by the Baker's Man, who was busy plying his trade. He was a very sweaty and incredibly hairy man. For a moment, the Cheese quietly surveyed the room. The captivating smells of maple bars and donuts were almost too much for the detective, and his stomach rumbled audibly in the cramped and dingy kitchen. Finally, he cleared his throat.

"Excuse me. I'm Detective Rodney Cheese, BCPD," he said. "I'm looking for some information about the murder last night."

The Baker's Man looked up from his work. "Sorry, I don't know nothin'," he said. He continued to go about his business as he spoke, rolling out a round of crust for a plum pie. He worked earnestly as if the pie were every bit as important as the murder investigation.

"Is that right?" said the Cheese. "Well, I know a few things. For instance, I've been here for all of two minutes and I've already spotted over fifteen health and safety violations. You know you're supposed to refrigerate eggs, right?"

"I guess so," the Baker's Man said with a shrug.

"You guess so? And would it kill you to wear a hairnet? I'll bet one of your sponge cakes has more hair than a French poodle."

"So?" said the Baker's Man.

"So? So you better start singing like four and twenty blackbirds baked in a pie or I'll have the health department shut you down faster than you can say *rub-a-dub-dub, three men in a tub*. Do I make myself clear?"

"Uh . . . yeah, pretty much," said the Baker's Man. "Well, except for the part about the three guys in the tub. That kind of threw me a little. Otherwise, I think I get it."

"Good," said the Cheese. "Now start spilling it like peas porridge in the pot nine days old before I lose my temper."

"Okay. I'll tell you everything I remember," said the Baker's Man. "It was about six o'clock, and I was baking a cake as fast as I could. Rush order. Wedding cake for the Dish and the Spoon. The bakery down the street refused to serve them, but I don't discriminate here. Anyway, I had the cake all mixed, and I was just about to pat it and prick it and mark it with a *B* and put it in the oven for a reasonable fee, when all of a sudden I heard a loud argument coming from Larry's place next door."

"Argument?" said the Cheese, trying to remain focused despite the wonderful confluence of smells. "What about?"

"It was all kind of garbled," said the Baker's Man. He folded the dough round in quarters, then placed it into a pie dish and unfolded it once more. "I heard this voice say something like, '*How dare you help a man like Krool. He's a murderer, and you are a traitor to the king.*' Guy was pretty upset."

"Then what happened?"

"I heard a scream and then nothing, so I figured the argument was over." The Baker's Man walked to the sink and began washing some plums. "But when I went out to the alley to take out the trash, I saw a guy running out the Muffin Man's back door."

"And this guy?" said the Cheese. "Can you describe him?"

"Don't have to describe him," said the Baker's Man. "I know exactly who it was. It was Jack."

"Jack?" repeated the Cheese with a quizzical frown. "You mean Jack B. Nimble?"

"No, no. The other one."

"Little Jack Horner?"

"No, the other Jack."

"Jack Sprat?"

"No, no." The Baker's Man was becoming increasingly frustrated. "You know who I'm talking about. *Jack*."

The Cheese thought long and hard. There was only one other Jack in all of Banbury Cross, but he was definitely not someone who would be involved in a murder. "You mean Jill's husband?"

"Yes," said the Baker's Man, snapping his fingers. "That's the guy."

"Are you sure?"

"Never been more sure about anything in my life," said the Baker's Man as he carried the plums to a cutting board. "Ran right by me."

Despite the certainty of the witness, the Cheese insisted on a full description, and the Baker's Man provided a detailed account of how the suspect looked, sounded, and even smelled.

"Oh. And one more thing," he added. "I'm not sure if this will be helpful or not, but when he ran by, I noticed that his clothes were covered in muffin batter."

The Cheese just stared at the man with a look of incredulity. If he'd had a head he would surely have been shaking it in disbelief. "What do you mean, you don't know if it'll be helpful?" he said. "Somebody drowns a guy in muffin mix, then you see a man running from the scene of the crime covered in the stuff and you're not sure whether that little bit of information might be helpful? Seriously?"

In addition to the Baker's Man's account, the Cheese canvassed the neighborhood and found others who told a story eerily similar in detail. One of those people was Carol Sprat, a large woman with an insatiable appetite for baked goods.

At first the woman was reluctant to admit she had been in the area because it was in direct defiance of orders from her doctor, who had cautioned Carol to cut back on simple carbohydrates. But when Detective Cheese pressed her, she revealed that she had been on the corner of Fifty-Fourth and Mulberry at the time of the murder to pick up a dozen day-old crullers, a bag of biscuits, and a double-fudge chocolate cake.

"And a few assorted Danishes," she added. "And some butter tarts."

Her husband, Jack, sat quietly at the kitchen table of their Lower East Side apartment eating a watercress salad while Carol attacked a canned ham with ferocity. The Cheese listened intently to her account of that evening's events, taking mental notes, only because he lacked the hands necessary to take actual notes.

"As I was walking back I heard a loud argument coming from inside the muffin shop," Carol mumbled. She knew it was rude for one to talk and eat at the same time, but the problem was that, at that moment, she didn't really want to stop doing either of those things. "Then I almost dropped my biscuits when I saw a man running out of the shop. He nearly bumped right into me."

"And did you recognize the man?"

Carol nodded yes, having just taken a bite of cured meat so large that it made speaking entirely impossible. "It was Jack," she said finally, with a gulp. "Not my husband, of course. The other one."

Jack Sprat nodded and smiled but said nothing and continued nibbling at his salad.

"You mean Jill's husband," confirmed the Cheese.

"Yes," said Carol, who then went on to describe the man she saw in the exact way that the Baker's Man had.

"I see," said the Cheese. "Anything else?"

"Well," said Carol, chewing and thinking with equal effort. "There is one more thing. I'm not sure if this will be of any use to you, but as he ran away, I noticed his clothes were covered in muffin batter."

The Cheese sighed heavily. "I swear this job is gonna kill the Cheese."

The weary detective left the Sprats' apartment and the Lower East Side behind and returned to the station to begin filling out a report with a heavy heart, for Jack was his friend and the father of Lady Elspeth the Conqueror. But it was beginning to look more and more that he was also a murderer.

Pat-a-cake, pat-a-cake, Baker's Man,
Give your account the best that you can.
Share it and swear it and mark it with a B,
And put it on record for the BCPD.

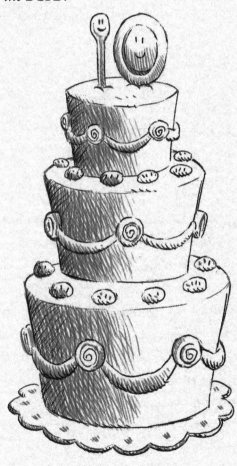

Chapter
12

Elspeth and the others had been on the road to St. Ives approaching two hours, and though the mood remained somber, it had grown less tense as the group had yet to fall victim to an ambush and Krool had made no attempt at escape. In fact, up to this point, the mission had gone exactly according to plan, which was either a very good sign or too good to be true.

The road was not nearly so wide out here in the grasslands and would allow the horses to travel only two abreast. None of them but Krool knew exactly where they were heading, so he naturally took the point with Cory riding to his right while his two equally muscle-bound brothers followed closely behind, their hands no longer on the grips of their swords as they had been at the start of the journey.

They rode silently except to lean toward one another on occasion and whisper and nod surreptitiously. Beyond having grown up in a shoe and their obsession with bodybuilding, Elspeth knew very little about the brothers, who often seemed sullen and brooding.

Riding behind them was Winkie, his head bobbing forward, his eyes closed. Stress-related insomnia in recent nights and the gentle swaying of the horse had finally induced sleep, and he snored as softly as you would expect of a man who was no bigger than a sack of flour. By comparison, Bo-Peep rode at the king's side, her eyes in keen and constant movement along the horizon, looking for danger of any kind. Years of tending sheep, watching for wolves and coyotes, had served to sharpen her senses.

Bringing up the rear were Dumpty, Elspeth, and, of course, Gene, who, in direct contrast to Bo-Peep's stoic Shaolin fighting stick, had been filling the air with noise fairly nonstop for the better part of an hour, most of it directly related to the mistreatment of sticks and trees.

"You know, they say you can tell how old a tree is by counting its rings," he griped. "Of course you can't do that without cutting the tree down. How ridiculous is that? I mean, they don't do that with people. '*Hey, how old is Grandpa? I don't know, let's chop him in half and find out.*' It's barbaric."

Gene huffed when he received not so much as a grunt in response. "What, am I talking to myself here?"

"Sorry, Gene," said Elspeth. "I've got a few other things on my mind, as I'm sure you can appreciate. I'm worried sick about Farrah."

"So am I," said Gene. "And I tend to get a little chatty when I'm stressed out."

"You don't say," said Dumpty.

"I just wish I knew more about this Mary Mary person," said Elspeth. "It would be helpful to have some idea as to what makes her tick."

"What makes her tick," said Dumpty, "is pure evil."

"Yes, but why?" said Elspeth. "What makes people like her and Krool choose to be that way?"

"Most likely, they were born evil," offered Dumpty.

"No," said Elspeth. "I'm sorry, but I have to disagree with you on that. After all, I should know. I used to be a little bit evil myself. For me, I think it was due to unhappiness. Before I came here I was a miserable person, and I worked hard to make sure everyone around me was just as miserable."

"Come now, you're exaggerating," said Dumpty. "When you first came to us you were unhappy to be sure. And a bit of a jackanapes perhaps, but not evil."

"That's what you think," said Gene. "The first time I met her she tossed me into a patch of weeds, which I did not appreciate. Neither did the weeds, as I recall."

"Just a reminder," said Elspeth, "that there are plenty of weeds around here too."

Gene chuckled nervously. "She's joking, of course."

"I am joking," she reassured the stick. "Now, that would be evil."

"So am I to understand, Elspeth," said Dumpty, "that you take the position that Mary Mary's evil tendencies are a result of some level of unhappiness?"

"I don't know," said Elspeth. "I think it may have something to do with it. Anyway, I guess it doesn't really matter. The more important question is, what gives her the power to carry out such evil?"

"What gives her the power," said Dumpty, "is the golden pear."

"What golden pear?" asked Elspeth.

Dumpty explained that years ago, when he was still a young half man, half egg, there stood in the town square a little nut tree given to the people of Banbury Cross as a gift from King William the Umpteenth's predecessor, King William the Bajillionth.

And though it seemed like an odd gift at the time, it turned out to be just the thing to bring the townspeople together. As years passed it became a ritual that every fall they would gather around the tree and harvest its bounty in a spirit of true community.

"It was a grand old party," said Dumpty. "With nuts everywhere.

"But more and more, as the years went by, people began to quarrel over the nuts, and there were those who took far more than their fair share, resulting in verbal and physical altercations."

"People fought over nuts?" asked Elspeth skeptically. After all, there were so many kids in her school with nut allergies that she could more easily imagine people fighting with them, as weapons, rather than about them.

"People will fight over rusty nails if they think someone is getting more than they are," said Dumpty. "And the more the people fought over the nuts, the more nuts the tree produced, until the harvest was no longer a grand old party but a scourge upon the village. And so the king ordered the tree chopped down and burned for firewood."

"Well, isn't that just the way," said Gene. "The people can't stop fighting over the tree, so what do they do? Do they get rid of the people? No, they chop down the tree. Hey, at least they could count the rings and find out how many years they'd been acting like complete jerks."

"I agree it was an absurd and entirely unfair solution to the problem," said Dumpty. "But in its place the king planted a second nut tree and ordered that its fruit must never be harvested. Anyone attempting to do so would meet a horrible fate. For years this was not an issue because the tree bore no fruit at all and served only to beautify the town square and provide shade in the summer months.

"Then one day, a crowd had gathered around the tree to witness a miracle. Hanging from its branches were a silver nutmeg and a pear made of solid gold. That a nut tree would spawn a pear and a nutmeg was, in and of itself, quite astonishing. That they were made of silver and gold was almost beyond belief. Now immediately the townspeople began to argue about whether the pear and the nutmeg should be plucked from the tree and used to enrich the village in some way.

"Ultimately none of them were willing to tempt fate. However, everyone knows that whatever is not harvested from a fruit-bearing tree will eventually fall to the ground on its own, so the townspeople crowded around the tree and waited. They slept beneath the tree and fought over the space closest to its trunk, each hoping to be the one to catch its bounty when it would finally succumb to gravity.

"One morning, they woke to find that the pear was missing, which set each and every villager against the other. The fighting and backbiting continued until it was discovered that, in addition to the pear being missing, so was one of the villagers."

"Let me guess," said Elspeth. "Mary Mary?"

"Exactly," said Dumpty.

Just then a flock of blackbirds took flight all at once

from the branches of a nearby maple tree, and the concert of flapping wings jolted Winkie from his catnap on horseback.

"What? Are we there?" he mumbled while smacking his dry lips together. "Have we gotten to the money?"

"Not yet," said Bo-Peep. "But we must be getting close by now. Assuming, that is, that the money actually exists."

"It had better exist," said Elspeth. "Or we'll drag Krool back to the village and let the mob deal with him."

"It exists, I assure you," said Krool, speaking over his shoulder.

As they crested a small hill, the tiny town of St. Ives came into view in the distance, and Elspeth drew in a deep breath. Her nostrils twitched at the smell of the cool sea air, which instantly reminded her of home. She closed her eyes and imagined sitting wharfside with her father, eating fish and chips while anticipating the ice cream in a waffle cone that always followed. It wasn't something they did often. Or at least not often enough. It was a special treat for when Sheldon had a particularly good month of sales.

And on those occasions when things had gone really well, they would walk down to Pike Place Market and explore the warren of ramps and corridors, stopping to marvel at the size of the Alaskan king crab legs or to duck into the vintage poster shop where Elspeth was allowed to pick out something that her mother would invariably find tasteless and inappropriate.

So there were some good things about the Deadlands, Elspeth decided. Things she missed and hoped to have a chance to experience again if she were able to make it out of this situation alive.

She inhaled once more and was amazed that the smell of one thing could summon the memories of so many others. And with equal efficiency, the sound of one thing quickly pushed those memories aside. That one thing was Gene, who had decided he'd been quiet for long enough.

"You know I've been considering a career change," he blurted into the near silence. "I think I'd make a really good scrub brush handle. I'm long, sturdy, and hard-working. All I need is a brush. Friend of mine did that. You know how much money he makes working from home now?"

"No idea," said Elspeth.

"Me neither," said Gene. "But I'll bet it's a lot."

"Speaking of money," said Winkie. "Where is it, Krool? I think we've gone far enough."

"If we'd gone far enough," Krool replied, "we'd be there by now, wouldn't we? I swear, you're as short on patience as you are on height."

Winkie seethed, staring daggers at the back of Krool's head, covered in thick, black hair. The only thing the king disliked more than bald jokes were short jokes, especially those delivered by someone so smug and so insufferably handsome.

"It's right up here," said Krool. "And I trust I don't have to remind you that we have an agreement in writing that is ironclad."

"You don't have to remind me," said Winkie. "That is one thing I will never forget as long as I live."

"Good," said Krool. "See that tree over there?"

Krool pointed ahead and off to the left where, standing next to a white, speckled boulder, there was something that looked as though it used to be a tree. Gray from the near constant barrage of salt and water, it was completely bare of bark, free of branches, and devoid of life. What remained of it extended only about ten feet from the ground. Erosion had exposed its roots to the point that daylight could be seen beneath them in places.

Krool turned off the road, and his horse trotted across the grass toward the tree and the rest of the group followed. Krool alit from his mount. The horse shuddered and seemed glad to be rid of him as the former prisoner walked closer to the tree. "Would you mind if I borrowed your little stick?" he said, extending a hand in Bo-Peep's direction. "Always a good idea to test for the presence of snakes before plunging your hand into a hole in the ground."

Slowly and reluctantly, Bo-Peep handed Krool her staff, the very one that had been used in battle against him. "Well, look at this," he said, slapping the stick forcefully into his palm. "In the right hands, a deadly weapon."

Then he abruptly turned toward the tree and repeatedly thrust the stick into the hole beneath its weathered roots. With each stabbing motion his jaw tightened and his face reddened. Finally, he finished, satisfied that if there were any snakes in the hole, they were now sufficiently tenderized.

Slightly out of breath from the assault, he walked back to Bo-Peep and handed her the stick with a slight bow of his head, so subtle that whether it was sincere or meant to mock could not be discerned. He returned to the tree and knelt down, and then reached into the hole. With a grunt he pulled forth a large burlap sack that clanked as it bumped its way into daylight.

"That doesn't sound like twenty thousand one-hundred-sixpence notes," said Winkie. "Is this some kind of a trick?"

"The trick," said Krool, "would be trying to keep all those bills dry in a burlap sack buried in a hole near the ocean."

Rory, Cory, and Maury gripped their sword handles as Krool loosened a tie at the end of the bag. They pulled those swords nearly half out of their scabbards as Krool reached into the bag and removed a glass jar. Inside that jar was what appeared to be a large roll of cash.

"Twenty jars each, with approximately one hundred thousand sixpence," he laughed. "But don't take my word for it. Here. Count it."

With an underhand motion Krool tossed Bo-Peep the jar. She looked carefully at the contents of the jar then tossed it back to Krool.

"You count it."

"Yes," said Krool. "Perhaps it's best. Numbers this large are not commonly known to people of your social standing."

Krool took his time, removing the cash from each jar, one by one, and counting its contents before returning the bills and sealing the lids once more. When he finished, the total was just over two million sixpence, just as Krool had promised. Once again, Elspeth thought that this was either very good news or too good to be true.

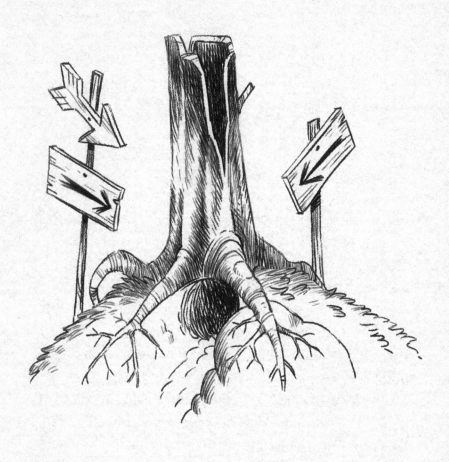

Hickory, dickory, dock,
A tree right next to a rock.
Beneath the roots,
Krool found the loot.
Hickory, dickory, dock.

Chapter
13

The group stood around the jars, placed in orderly rows upon the ground, while the horses, having little regard for money, ate grass and talked quietly among themselves about things of interest to them, such as eating grass.

"Well then," said Krool, rubbing his palms together. "I must say it's been a pleasure doing business with you all. I suppose there's nothing left to do now but to divvy it up and go our separate ways."

Reluctant as he may have been to hand Krool his freedom along with a small fortune, Winkie was also anxious to be moving on to the second phase of the mission— bringing his wife safely home to the castle. "Yes," he agreed. "I suppose so."

Suddenly, the sharp sound of swords being pulled from scabbards filled the air.

"I don't think so," said Cory. He and his brothers circled Krool with the casual swagger of people who clearly have the upper hand. "That money belongs to us now."

Krool focused his response not on the brothers but on King William. "And just what is the meaning of this, Winkie? This is how you honor a written agreement?"

"I have nothing to do with this, I assure you," Winkie responded. "Gentlemen, explain yourselves."

"He destroyed our home," said Cory, nearing tears.

"I know that," said Winkie. "And I'm very sorry for you."

"Yes, but what you don't know is that the other kids made fun of us because we always smelled like the inside of a shoe," said Rory.

"Kids can be so cruel," said Gene with a *tsk-tsk*.

"So we started lifting weights to compensate for our feelings of inadequacy," explained Maury. "Now we can't stop. For goodness' sake, look at the size of my neck!"

"I have to walk through doors sideways," said Cory.

"We have to have our clothes custom made," said Rory.

"And that costs money," said Cory. "So we're taking this because we need it and because it's rightfully ours."

Winkie let out a sigh and looked upon the brothers with pity. "Listen, fellas," he said. "Look at me. I'm bald as an egg. No offense, Dumpty."

"None taken," said Dumpty.

"And I'm so short I once got kicked in the face by a

cockapoo," Winkie continued. "True story. What I'm say-ing is, I know what it's like to struggle with self-image."

"We all do," said Elspeth. "I used to speak with a terri-ble lisp. The other kids would call me Sylvester the cat."

"Kids used to roll me down the hill and into the pond," said Dumpty.

"Try being a girl growing up with a name like Bo," said Bo-Peep.

"And what about me?" said Krool. "Do you think I was born this way? Intelligent, charming, and incredibly handsome? Well, I was, so I can't really relate. Still, I'm sure that having to grow up in a shoe was very traumatic for you."

"Yes," agreed Winkie. "And I promise that when we return we'll get you the counseling you need, free of charge. But right now all that matters is that I've signed a legally binding contract with Krool."

"You have," said Maury. "But we haven't."

"That may be so," Dumpty interjected. "But may I remind you that you entered into an equally binding contract with your king when you swore your oath of allegiance. It is a sacred vow that must never be broken."

"But that's different," Rory objected. "Of course we honor our vow to King William. But how can we abide by a contract with a monster like this?"

Whereas most people might have been offended at such characterization, Krool seemed almost flattered by it.

"You will abide by it because you must," said Winkie. "As unpalatable as it might be, the rule of law must be respected above all else if a society is to remain civilized. Now, I could order you, as your sovereign, to put your weapons away and stand down. But I would prefer to ask you. Gentlemen? Please, would you kindly sheath your weapons?"

The three brothers looked at one another and then at the jars full of money, and then at Krool, who fought his instinct to make a snide remark and wisely kept his mouth shut.

Cory was the first to concede and the others followed, slamming their swords into their scabbards with force backed by anger and frustration. A satisfied smile and a sense of relief spread out across Krool's angular face.

"Thank you," said Winkie. "As hard as it might be to fathom, you boys are doing the right thing."

"Yes," said Krool. "And don't worry. No hard feelings."

"All right then," said Winkie quickly. "Let's get down to business here. After all, it's getting late."

No sooner had he uttered these words then there came a low, whirring sound off in the direction from which they'd come. Turning toward the noise, each of them was aghast at the sight they beheld. It was a torcano coming directly for them at an alarming speed. So quickly was the towering funnel of flame approaching that there was no time to grab the cash or to mount the horses. There was time for only one thing.

"Run!" shouted Winkie, and run they did, the horses and the humans, some scattering to the left, some to the right, giving as much way as possible to the torcano, its volume level increasing to jet engine strength as it swooped in.

Krool and Dumpty sought cover behind the old tree. The three brothers hit the ground and rolled into a shallow ditch. Winkie hid behind a small shrub named Kent, while Bo-Peep and Elspeth, with Gene in hand, dove headfirst behind the white-speckled boulder, as the churning whirlwind of fire grew louder and nearer.

"What is a torcano doing way out here?" Elspeth shouted. "We're nowhere near Torcano Alley."

"I don't know," Bo-Peep yelled back.

"Maybe it's lost," hollered Gene.

Bits of rock and dirt rained down upon them. Though it was better than being out in the open, a boulder would provide little protection if the torcano suddenly changed course and veered even slightly in their direction.

Elspeth hunched her shoulders and crouched down as far as she could manage. She remembered her promise to Jack and Jill that everything would be okay, and she feared now that it was a promise she might not be able to keep. Having survived two torcanoes in the past, what were the odds of emerging from a third unscathed? And just as she resigned herself to the fact that she might not make it out of this one alive, the noise quite abruptly ceased as if the torcano had been suddenly switched off like an electric fan.

"It stopped," Elspeth whispered. She had never known a torcano to behave in such a way. A sour smell drifted through the air and found its way to her nostrils.

Slowly, Bo-Peep and Elspeth and Gene inched upward, peering over the top of the boulder. The torcano had completely disappeared but for a small cloud of smoke, hovering close to the ground directly over those jars of cash.

When a sudden breeze dispersed the cloud, they saw an unspeakably hideous woman standing in its place. The sleeves of her white dress were torn, and the hem hung in tatters around her feet. Her stark white hair was thick, matted, and twisted, protruding from her head in all directions. Her skin was a ghostly gray. Dark circles framed her milky-white eyes that dripped with a thick yellow acid. Her lips were black and curled into a self-satisfied grin. From a rusted iron chain about her neck hung a golden pear, the sunlight playing off its polished surface.

Just to look at the woman made Elspeth feel instantly sick to her stomach. "Is that—?"

"Mary Mary," Bo-Peep whispered back.

"Wow," said Gene. "She's really let herself go."

Despite having let herself go, there was nothing wrong with the woman's ears as her head snapped in the direction of Gene's voice and her murky eyes landed upon Elspeth—or so it seemed. It's difficult to tell exactly where an eye with no iris is aimed. Still, it was close enough to cause Elspeth and Bo-Peep to duck back down behind the rock.

From there they could hear the clinking of glass as Mary Mary quickly filled the burlap sack with the jars of cash and then slung the bag over her shoulder.

"She's taking the money," Bo-Peep whispered.

Gene scoffed loudly. "Ha! Over Elspeth's dead body she is."

"What?" said Elspeth.

"Well, you're not just going to sit here and do nothing, are you? Come on. Where's that kick-butt attitude?"

"Right," said Elspeth.

"No," said Bo-Peep. "Don't do it. It's not safe."

But it was too late. Elspeth's fear proved a poor match for her pride, and without further thought she sprang to her feet. "Hey!" she shouted in the direction of the witch.

The witch replied with an otherworldly hiss, which resulted in a thick, burgundy-colored steam escaping her ebony lips. Elspeth realized her hands were trembling, though she couldn't be sure if it was the result of her own fear or of the shivering stick she was holding.

"Okay," said Gene. "I think you got her attention. Let's go back behind the rock now."

Not only did Elspeth not return to her hiding place but her fellow travelers, in a show of solidarity, emerged from theirs as well. Bo-Peep stood beside her while the three brothers crawled out of the ditch and King William stepped out from behind the shrub.

"You!" he said, successfully diverting the witch's attention from Elspeth. "You've gotten your money. So as your king, I demand the safe return of Queen Farrah without further delay. Do you hear me?"

Mary Mary hissed again, expelling another cloud of what looked like breath mixed with blood. She pushed a slender finger in Winkie's direction. From the tip of the finger came a flash of white light that sliced through the air with the speed of a diving falcon. Winkie lunged to one side just as the light hit Kent, causing the shrub to explode instantly, leaving nothing but charred twigs where he'd once stood. Gene gasped in horror, and Winkie looked at the former bush realizing he'd previously had no idea what he was dealing with.

The witch pointed at Winkie once more and seemed for a very long moment to be considering her options. Winkie, on the other hand, had few options of his own but to stand still and hope. And just when he thought it a foregone conclusion that he, like Kent, would be blasted into oblivion, the witch quite abruptly swung around until that same finger was trained on the horses, huddled together on the slope of a small hill.

"No!" shouted Winkie. "Not the horses!"

His words did nothing to stop the light—a bright pink this time—that rocketed forth from Mary Mary's finger. Elspeth winced in anticipation of the horses being instantly incinerated. But when the light struck them they were not reduced to ashes but rather transformed. No longer were they eight horses but eight armadillos—and not just armadillos, but pink armadillos wearing small armadillo-size saddles.

Then the witch hissed again, lowered her hand, and began spinning, slowly at first, then building up speed like a figure skater, until the mog had transmogrified, once more, into a torcano.

Elspeth and the others watched, helpless, silent, and astonished, as Mary Mary, along with the twelve million pence, whirled away, across the grassy plain, in the general direction of the Thick.

"Arrrgh!" Krool bellowed as he ran to the place where the jars of money had sat only moments before. "This is not happening!" He screamed with enough force to hurt his throat. Veins bulged from his forehead, which had turned a deep red, approaching purple. "Come back here this minute! How dare you steal my stolen loot!"

The armadillos, having no more regard for money than when they were horses, ate bugs and talked quietly among themselves about things of interest to them, such as eating bugs.

One by one, the others joined Krool in staring disbelievingly at the spot of bare ground and the concentric circles the spinning witch had left in the dirt.

"So that was it," said Elspeth. "I knew this whole thing seemed too good to be true."

"I told you she was a mog," said Gene. "She can take on the form of just about anything."

Krool turned to the three brothers with rage in his eyes. "You!" he said through grinding teeth. "This is all your fault."

"Our fault?" said Cory.

"That's right. If you hadn't slowed things down by trying to steal my stolen loot, then that nasty old witch never would have had the time to steal it. I would've been long gone by the time she showed up, on my way to sipping a piña colada on the beach."

"How dare you?" said Dumpty, placing himself between Krool and the three boys. "How dare you accuse these lads of such a thing? If you hadn't stolen the money in the first place, we wouldn't have had to come here and retrieve it."

"You listen to me, Dumpty," sneered Krool. "You would do well to remember that eggs are meant to be beaten."

By force of habit, Dumpty brought his hand to the side of his face and ran it along the scars, present and permanent as a result of a ruthless beating at the hands of Krool's former henchmen.

139

Before Krool could speak again, he felt the thrust of a stick to the sternum as Bo-Peep pushed him away from Dumpty and moved her face very close to his. "First of all, he's not an egg, he's a man, which is more than I can say for you. And if you ever threaten him again, I'll make sure that you wish you hadn't."

"Yeah, take that!" said Gene.

Krool snapped his head in Gene's direction. "You might want to think about minding your own business," he growled. "Or you may very well find yourself in a wood chipper."

"Quiet!" yelled Elspeth. "Enough. We're wasting valuable time here. The fact of the matter is that this is nobody's fault. Mary duped us all, plain and simple."

"She's right," said Krool. "We've been had. Now we can sit around feeling sorry for ourselves, blubbering like a child with a boo-boo on his knee, or we can get moving."

"We?" said Bo-Peep, making no effort to hide her disgust. "Unfortunately we have a contract that prohibits us from throwing you back in prison. So, for all intents and purposes, our dealings with you are finished."

"You may be finished with me," said Krool, "but I'm going to get my money back if it's the last thing I do. Nobody steals from Jonathan Ellington Rutherford Krool and gets away with it. So like it or not, I'm going where you're going. And you're going where I'm going. Now, we can split up and seek to achieve our goals separately, or we can travel together and help each other."

"Sorry, but we have no interest in your kind of help," said Dumpty.

"Pity," said Krool. "Because my kind of help is exactly what you need."

"What do you mean?" asked Elspeth.

"I think you would agree that when it comes to Mary Mary, you're dealing with pure evil," said Krool. "And the only way to fight pure evil is to understand how it works and why it does what it does. Who better to provide that insight than someone who has made evil his life's work?"

Winkie looked at his trusted advisors, one by one, to see if their faces might reveal how they felt about adding another advisor into the mix, especially one so vile and corrupt. "I don't know. What do you think?"

"To take advice in regard to strategy from a man like Krool I believe is a horrible idea," said Dumpty.

"Then again," added Elspeth, "a horrible idea is better than no idea at all."

Bo-Peep stared at Krool with a searing hatred then back to Winkie, her look quickly softening. "I agree with Elspeth," she said. "In this situation, the worst kind of help is better than none."

"And you," Winkie said to the brothers. "What do you boys feel about all this?"

The brothers exchanged looks among themselves then seemed to decide that Cory would be the one to answer on their behalf. "As Mr. Dumpty said, we've sworn an oath to serve Your Majesty. How we feel about it doesn't really matter."

"It does matter," said Winkie. "It matters to me. So please, speak freely."

"Well," said Cory. "To be honest, I think it stinks. I mean, first we have to give him a full pardon and release him from prison. Then we have to abide by some ridiculous contract. Now we have to travel with him? And work together with him?"

"So you're opposed to the idea," said Winkie.

"No," said Cory. "We're in favor of anything that might help bring the queen back safely. But make no mistake about it. It stinks."

"I agree," said Dumpty.

"Well," said Krool. "That's the important thing now, isn't it? That we all agree. Now let's get moving here." Then, with a faint smile and an eye on Dumpty, he added, "Last one there is a rotten egg."

Mary ran a little scam, little scam, little scam,
Mary ran a little scam and fleeced King William so.
Everything, twelve million pence, million pence, million pence,
Everything, twelve million pence, she took back to her home.

She also swindled Krool that day, Krool that day, Krool that day,
She also swindled Krool that day, just like an April fool.
It was enough to make him say, make him say, make him say,
It was enough to make him say, "That's totally uncool."

Chapter 14

As Elspeth and her disheartened crew made their way toward the Thick, back in Banbury Cross, Jack and Jill went up the hill to fetch a pound of butter, a loaf of bread, a dozen eggs, and some other items they needed from the various shops in town. On the way back, they talked, as they frequently did, about Elspeth.

"I can't believe she would lie to us like that," Jack said. "She promised us she was here only in an advisory capacity."

"I doubt she lied to us so much as changed her mind," Jill replied. "Or was coerced into it."

"Still, I should have ordered her not to go," said Jack, the regret carved out in the lines upon his weathered face.

"You don't know your own daughter very well if you think that would've stopped her."

"It would've been worth a shot. Dealing with a powerful witch like Mary Mary is much too dangerous for a child her age."

"More dangerous than leading an armed rebellion against an evil tyrant?" Jill answered.

"I don't know," said Jack. "Maybe not. But we probably shouldn't have let her do that either."

"Then we'd all still be living out in the slums, eating peas porridge every day, while Krool continued his reign of terror," Jill reminded him.

"Still," said Jack, "what kind of parent puts his child in such danger just so he can eat a little better?"

"It was more than that and you know it," said Jill. "It was the fulfillment of the prophecy, the realization of her destiny."

"Yes, I know," Jack agreed. "Either way, I won't be able to sleep until she's back here safe and sound."

"Well," said Jill, "at least I can enjoy the lack of snoring for a few nights."

When Jack did not laugh in response or offer even so much a gap-toothed smile, Jill knew there was more on his mind. "What are you thinking, Jack?"

"I've made a decision," he said. "I'm going after her. It's my duty as her father to be there should she need me. I will leave first thing tomorrow morning."

"But this is official royal business," said Jill. "And the king didn't authorize you to go."

"A so-called king once stopped me from protecting

my child," said Jack. His face was rigid and stern now. "And my lack of backbone resulted in her being thrown down a well. Never will I let something like that happen again."

If there was one thing Jill knew about her husband, besides the fact that he snored quite loudly and on a nightly basis, was that he was very stubborn. Once he'd made his mind up about something, there was very little chance of dissuading him.

"But what if something happens to you?" She took his right arm in both hands and pulled him close as they walked.

"I'm a grown man," said Jack. "I can fend for myself."

Jill remained silent for a time then said, "If you go, I'm going with you."

"Absolutely not," said Jack. "I forbid it."

Jill raised an eyebrow and looked up at Jack with both annoyance and amusement. "You forbid it? Did you really just say that?"

"I'm sorry," said Jack. He hung his head and gave it a shake. "I didn't mean that. I just don't think it would be a good idea, considering the circumstances. That's all."

As they neared their tiny cottage, the conversation abruptly ended when they were greeted by a sight that in the Deadlands would have been quite perplexing. Even here in New Winkieland it was a bit hard to imagine why a giant wheel of cheese was standing at their front door, beneath the eaves of the house.

"Hey, Jack," said the Cheese as Jack and Jill turned from the road onto the stone walkway, lined with white and pink roses still in bloom in the late summer warmth. "How you doing?"

"Great," said Jack, suddenly filled with a sense of panic. After all, his daughter had set out on a dangerous mission earlier that day and now an officer of the law was standing on his stoop. He feared the Cheese might be bearing news of a parent's worst nightmare. Having lost Elspeth once before, he knew his heart could not endure such a thing again. "What is it, Rodney?" His voice quavered slightly despite his best efforts to appear nonchalant. "To what do we owe this visit?"

"You mind if I come in?" said the Cheese.

"Sure," said Jack, his unease growing with each passing second.

"Is everything okay?" asked Jill, not to be outworried by her husband. "Is Elspeth all right?"

"I hope so," said the Cheese. "Haven't heard anything to the contrary. Actually, I'm here about another matter."

With a sigh of relief, Jack opened the door, and he and Jill carried the groceries to the kitchen and placed them on the round oak table for the moment.

The Cheese followed them in, rolling across the cozy living room. The tiny windows provided only thin streaks of light in the otherwise shady cottage. All about were reminders for the Cheese that he was in the home of the parents of a living legend. There were pictures of the girl hanging above the stone fireplace. On the mantel were trophies from chess tournaments that she'd won in the Deadlands and had brought back for her proud parents to put on display.

"May I offer you a cup of tea?" asked Jill.

That the Cheese politely declined the gesture further enforced Jack and Jill's feeling that this visit was not a social one.

"You mind telling me where you were two nights ago?" asked the Cheese, seemingly more interested in the inscription on one of the trophies than in the answer to his question. "Around six o'clock?" Displaying a lack of interest was a technique the Cheese had learned at the academy—a way of putting suspects at ease.

"Six o'clock," Jack said, pulling methodically at his chin. "Sorry, but my thoughts are a little muddled these days. I've got a lot on my mind."

"Don't sweat it," said the Cheese, now studying a photo of Elspeth posing with Queen Farrah. "Take your time."

"Let's see. As I recall, I went up the hill to fetch some flowers from the meadow. I wanted to surprise Jill when she got home from work. She loves the look of fresh wildflowers on the table."

"Plus it helps cover up the smell of trash," Jill added with a smile.

"It's not my fault." Jack pouted. "I bathe every day, but sometimes you just can't—"

"So you went alone," the Cheese confirmed.

"That's right."

"Anyone see you?"

"Not that I know of," said Jack. "What's this all about, anyway?"

The Cheese bit his lower lip and enjoyed the taste of it enough to continue a while before finally saying, "I got two witnesses who swear they saw you in the Baking District that night."

Jack frowned and shook his head decisively. "I was nowhere near the Baking District."

"They said they saw you running from the Muffin Man's place after a loud argument. And your clothes were covered in muffin batter, which, by the way, is a pretty important little detail."

"Well, they must be mistaken," Jack insisted. "Or lying."

"They were absolutely certain it was you they saw," said the Cheese. "And I can't think of a good reason for them to lie about that. So unless you have an evil twin—"

"Are you suggesting I had something to do with his murder?" Jack asked.

"*I'm* not suggesting it," said the Cheese. "The evidence is."

Jill gasped and leaned on the kitchen table to keep from falling over. Jack's face dropped and turned a sickly gray. "But it's me you're talking to," he said. "You know I would never do such a thing."

"Now listen," said the Cheese, rolling closer to his friend so he could lower his voice farther yet. "I know you're not the kind of guy to go out and commit premeditated murder. But let's say you found out the Muffin Man was supplying money to the guy who tried to kill your little girl. You got angry, went over there to have a word with him. Things got out of control. It happens."

"Not in this case it didn't," Jack protested.

A pained expression came over Detective Cheese's face, and he nodded slowly to the extent that a wheel of cheese can nod. "I'm sorry, Jack. But I'm afraid I'm gonna have to place you under arrest for the murder of Larry the Muffin Man."

Jack could think of nothing more to say other than to repeatedly and firmly deny any involvement in the crime. Still, he surrendered peacefully. He kissed Jill and held her tight while the Cheese waited, giving them as much time as they needed.

"Don't worry, it'll be okay," said Jack, finally breaking off the embrace. "It's all just a big mistake. We'll get this whole thing sorted, and I'll be home for dinner. Meat loaf would be nice."

"Sure," said Jill, that smile of hers trying so hard to remain reassuring. "Meat loaf it is."

Jack accompanied Detective Cheese to the police

department, where he was fingerprinted and booked on murder charges.

By the time the paperwork had been processed, Jack was almost too sick from it all to walk to the dungeon where he would await arraignment and his chance to enter a plea. Slowly, he began to lose hope of making it home in time for a meat loaf dinner as one by one the hours went by.

Coincidentally, he sat alone in the very cell in which he and Jill had been held for months when Krool found them to be enemies of the state by virtue of being the parents of the child prophesied to lead an uprising against him. The only difference this time was that Jack was alone in the cell. Oh yes, there was one more difference. This time there was also a rather smelly monkey in the cell across the way, staring at him with a big, creepy smile.

"What are you looking at?" Jack scowled. He sat on the cot, his elbows on his knees, chin resting on his hands, pushed together and balled up in fists. "I'm innocent."

The monkey only smiled a bigger and toothier smile then turned his back to Jack and bent over at the waist.

"That's incredibly rude," Jack said. "Didn't your mother teach you any manners? Anyway, why should I care what you think?"

Another hour slipped away before the sound of jangling keys echoed through the cellblock. The door to the dungeon opened and in walked a man who looked as though he had a habit of sleeping in his clothes. Or maybe it was a hobby. Either way, his hair stuck up in several places and there were lines across his left cheek, the kind often caused by lengthy contact with a pillow. He had a flat, leather satchel tucked beneath the arm of his rumpled blue suit.

He stopped in front of the cell housing the monkey and looked in. "Good afternoon, Jack," he said. "My name is Jack too. Jack B. Nimble of Nimble, Nimble, Tucker, and Levine. I'm your court-appointed attorney."

"Excuse me," said Jack. He raised his hand to make himself more visible in the dim light. "Over here. I'm Jack."

"Well, how about that?" said Nimble. "Three of us and all named Jack."

"No," said Jack. "I'm the guy you're looking for. As far as I know the monkey's name is Tad."

The monkey smiled and waved at Nimble.

"Tad?" said Nimble "Oh. Sorry." He moved across to Jack's cell then took a seat upon a wooden stool, slouching forward. He opened his satchel and removed a pencil and a stack of badly dog-eared papers. "Okay, then. Let's get right down to business. I see here you've been charged with murdering a muffin named Larry."

"Muffin *Man*," Jack corrected. "Larry the Muffin Man."

"Muffin Man," Nimble repeated with an air of intrigue as he scribbled with a pencil on the file. "So he's a man . . . but with all the powers of a muffin?"

"No. He's just a regular guy who drowned in a vat of muffin mix," said Jack.

Nimble snapped his fingers. "And that's how he got his super muffin powers?"

Jack groaned and threw up his hands. "No, no. He's just some guy who makes muffins. Or he used to be, before somebody killed him. Somebody who's not me."

"Ah, now I understand," said Nimble. "Sort of. Anyway, the bad news is the cops have several eyewitnesses who will swear they saw you running from the scene of the crime covered in muffin batter. They also have hair sample evidence and a footprint in the batter that matches the sole of your shoe."

"Okay," said Jack. "And what's the good news?"

Nimble's eyeballs rolled back in thought and stayed there for a moment. "I don't remember saying there was any good news," he said finally. "If I did, I apologize because there isn't. Now I suggest you agree to plead guilty in exchange for a lesser sentence."

"But I'm not guilty," said Jack. "Haven't you heard a word I've said? Now I've got to get out of here as soon as possible. My daughter might be in very grave danger. Besides, I'm the garbage man. If I'm locked up, who's going to collect the garbage?"

"Garbage man," said Nimble, suddenly correcting his posture. "So you're a regular man but with all the powers of garbage?"

Lacking the energy to refute such an absurd remark,

Jack just sighed heavily. "Yes," he said. "I have all the powers of garbage."

"Fascinating," said Nimble. "Now don't worry. We'll get you out of here. Just as soon as you post bail, which has been set at ten thousand sixpence."

"Ten thousand sixpence?" Jack exclaimed. "Where am I going to get that kind of money?"

"Well," said Nimble. "Perhaps your wife has some jewelry she could sell."

"Yes," said Jack sadly. "She has a necklace. I gave it to her on our twentieth wedding anniversary. I suppose that would do."

"Good," said Nimble. "And when you get out of here, I hope that from now on you'll use your super garbage powers for good and not evil."

Though it saddened Jill to remove the necklace from the tiny velvet-covered box on her dresser and take it down to the pawnshop, it was certainly better than sitting home alone with an anniversary gift in a box and a husband languishing in a box of his own.

Brother John's Trade and Pawn was a small, dark room cluttered with the material manifestations of broken dreams and waning hope. Layers of dust on the once-prized items stacked on shelves and displayed in glass cases made it clear that what many thought to be a good solution to a temporary problem had turned out to be nothing more than a tiny bandage on a wound that never healed.

There were tools and musical instruments and sporting equipment and, of course, plenty of jewelry.

As she walked in, Jill assumed that the man behind the counter was Brother John. A very round individual, he sat on a stool with his head down and eyes closed, his heavily tattooed forearms folded across his protruding belly.

When the ringing of the bell attached to the door failed to stir the man, Jill approached the counter and gently cleared her throat.

"Excuse me," she said softly. "Brother John? Are you sleeping?"

The man's eyes sprang open, and he looked around the room as though surprised to find that he was not someplace else.

"Hello," he said. "What is it? How can I help you today?"

"I have something to sell," Jill replied as she placed the necklace on the glass countertop.

With the chain pinched between his thumb and forefinger, Brother John lifted the necklace and held it up to the light, inspecting it carefully, with a well-trained and skeptical eye.

"Not bad," he snorted. "I can give you five thousand sixpence."

"But I need ten," said Jill, shocked to find the treasured gift so undervalued. Brother John lowered the necklace to the countertop. "Well, you got anything else to sell?"

"No," said Jill. "I'm afraid not."

Out of habit, Brother John glanced down at Jill's left hand. She flinched at the overfamiliarity when he grabbed her by the wrist and pulled her hand close to his face. "Not bad," he said, squinting sharply. "I could probably give you three thousand more for those."

Jill's eyes landed upon the wedding band and engagement ring that had been on her left hand for so long they felt more a part of her than an attachment. She pulled her hand away and wiped it on her dress.

"But I couldn't possibly sell them," she said.

"Then all I can give you is five thousand," said Brother John with what he probably thought was a sympathetic shrug.

Jill looked at the man then back at the rings, the physical embodiment of Jack's love for her and hers for him. Then she twisted and turned and slowly removed those rings that she could never imagine selling and placed them on the glass countertop next to the necklace.

I've got sweet bling, I've got sweet bling,
Brother John's Trade and Pawn.
I can sell you something,
A necklace and two gold rings.
Bling-bling gone, bling-bling gone.

Chapter 15

Because he had kept his part of the bargain by leading them to the money, Krool was now officially a free man. And if Elspeth and her friends thought Krool the prisoner was unbearably obnoxious, they now had to deal with Krool the fully pardoned and legally untouchable ex-con.

"Could we possibly pick up the pace here?" he growled. "At this rate, by the time we get where we're going, that awful witch will have spent half my money on hair spray and eye of newt."

This was more than likely an unfounded concern being that there were no hair salons, mini malls, or stores of any kind in the Thick. Besides, it was common knowledge that most witches bought their eye of newt in the bulk section of the local market.

Still, Krool was right about one thing. With the horses having been turned into armadillos, the traveling speed of the group had been greatly diminished by the fact that they now had to go on foot, carrying all the provisions on their own backs. For an elfin man like Winkie, on the other hand, such an animal offered the perfect ride.

"I can't believe you would allow yourself to be humiliated like this," Krool said, looking down on Winkie both literally and figuratively as he walked alongside him. "Aren't you worried what people are going to say about their king parading around on the back of a pink . . . whatever that thing is?"

"Armadillo," said the armadillo over its pink-armored shoulder. "And I'm not pink. I'm dusty rose."

"I don't care what your name is," said Krool. "Anyway, I suppose you'll come in handy should we run out of food."

The dusty-rose armadillo responded to the remark by belching loudly and returning to the more important task of filling its own belly, gobbling up any and all insects along the road. Beyond Krool's occasional snide remark, for a very long time there was little or no conversation among the group. Even Gene, after having seen an innocent shrub instantly reduced to cinders, had decided it was best to keep a much lower profile.

The silence from the others might have been due to fatigue after a long day of travel but most likely it was something not so easily remedied with a good night's sleep. Since that up-close encounter with Mary Mary, the general mood had changed from caution and trepidation to a steady and abiding fear. And though Elspeth was looked upon as a brave general and liberator of the people, inside she was absolutely terrified of what lay ahead. While it was true that she had experienced fear while leading an armed rebellion against Krool, this was entirely different. Toppling the wicked king and his army had been a dangerous undertaking, but at least Krool was bound by the laws of nature. Mary Mary, on the other hand, seemed to have command of them, the ability to bend and break them on a whim.

Elspeth wondered what other incredible things the witch could do. What, if any, were her limits and weaknesses? Just then, her thoughts were interrupted by a shadow moving quickly across the ground. Glancing up, she caught site of a hawk circling overhead. Was it just that? A hawk in search of field mice? Or was it Mary Mary, watching and stalking them from above?

"Do you think that's her?" asked Gene, terrified at the thought of being reduced to a glowing ember.

"I don't know," said Elspeth. She studied the bird as keenly as she could from such a distance. "Probably just a hawk. Still, it's best to be ready for anything."

"I'm ready for anything but spontaneous combustion," Gene replied.

And while Gene trembled in Elspeth's hand, there was another member of the group experiencing a far more severe reaction to the stress. The feeling that Mary Mary could strike at any time, from any angle, and in any number of incarnations soon became too much for Dumpty and caused his vertigo to return for the first time since Winkie had been restored to the throne. Without warning, he teetered one way and would have toppled right over the other way if Bo-Peep, with her cat-quick reflexes, hadn't reached out and caught him by the arm.

"Dumpty! Are you okay?" she exclaimed as he continued to wobble and she continued to fight to keep him on his feet.

"Just fine," he lied, while stumbling about. It would have been comical were it not so painful to watch a man struggle against a renewed feebleness he thought he'd long ago conquered. "No problem at all."

The three brothers rushed to Dumpty's side, took him by the elbows, and helped lower him to a seated position in the middle of the road. "Easy now, Mr. Dumpty," said Cory.

Dumpty shook his head, and his eyes gave several exaggerated blinks. "I'm so sorry," he said, feeling suddenly more ashamed than dizzy. "It's just the stress. I'll be fine in a moment or two."

Such a failure in front of his friends was humbling to

be sure. But to falter like this in the presence of Krool was nothing short of devastating.

"Well, it looks as though someone chose the wrong profession," said Krool, wasting no time in seizing upon the opportunity to further embarrass Dumpty. He stood over the fallen spy with his hands on his hips. "A secret agent who can't handle stressful situations. What's next? A tightrope walker who's afraid of heights?"

"Quiet, you insensitive animal," Elspeth scolded.

"Hey, I resent that," said the armadillo.

"Sorry," said Elspeth. "You're right. That was an unfair comparison."

Krool seemed amused by it all. After all, stirring things up had always been one of his favorite things to do. "I would like to assert that I am not entirely unsympathetic to Dumpty's situation," he said. "And if he's unable to walk any farther, I would be more than happy to roll him the rest of the way."

Bo-Peep stepped forward and held the end of her staff very close to Krool's square, dimpled chin. "If you're in such a hurry," she said, "then perhaps you'd better go on ahead. And if you choose to remain with us, you'd better have something to offer in exchange for us having to put up with your horrible attitude."

"Yes," said Winkie. He dismounted from the armadillo and walked back toward Dumpty and the others. "Let's hear it, Krool. I think it's time for you to put your stolen money where your foul mouth is and reveal your plan to deal with Mary Mary. Tell us, how do you propose we vanquish a witch with powers to turn a black horse into a pink armadillo?"

"Dusty rose," said the armadillo, though no one seemed to notice.

"It's quite simple," said Krool. He sauntered to the side of the road and took a seat upon a log that was too old to object to the intrusion. "If there's one thing I understand more than evil, it's greed. And the fact that Mary Mary would give up her youth and beauty for possession of a golden pear, and that she would not be content with the million sixpence ransom she originally demanded, tells me we're dealing with someone whose greed possibly rivals my own."

"Hard to imagine," said Elspeth.

"Yes, quite impressive, isn't it?" said Krool with the kind of admiration one boxer might show for another who has just beaten the stuffing out of him.

"Still, I fail to see how Mary Mary's greedy nature is of any benefit to us," said Winkie. "All it means is that there's no pleasing her."

"This is precisely why you need me more than you know," said Krool. "You see, to a point, greed is a strength." He spoke as if referring to the nutritional benefits of a high-fiber diet. "It propels people like me to great accomplishments. Without it I never would have become king. Of course, with anything, too much of it and that strength quickly becomes a weakness. When you over-extend yourself, entire empires can collapse. Just ask the Romans."

"A lovely history lesson, but your plan is still missing a great deal of detail," said Winkie. He walked over and climbed up onto the log on which Krool sat to better face him eye to eye.

"Actually, it's missing only one," said Krool. "Answer me this. What's the one thing that all greedy people want but can't buy?"

"A unicorn?" said Gene.

This earned Gene a scowl from Krool. Gene would have responded with a shrug if sticks had the shoulders necessary for such things. "No," Krool sneered. "Not a unicorn. I'm talking about power. Political power. In this case, the throne."

Winkie nearly tumbled off the log. "What? Are you suggesting I hand over the keys to the kingdom to some lunatic witch?"

"You don't hand them over," said Krool. "You dangle them in front of her, like raw meat before a tiger."

"I don't understand," said Winkie.

"Of course you don't," said Krool. "So allow me to explain it to you. Money, jewels, your precious queen. These are all things she can abscond with and take back to the Thick. But if you can convince her that she can have it all, and that she deserves nothing less, she'll have to come to you. Home-field advantage: Winkie."

The king stood in silence for a moment, his eyes narrowed in thought. "I don't know," he said. "What do you think, Dumpty?"

"I don't like it," Dumpty answered.

Krool sprang to his feet somewhat aggressively and threw up his hands. "Of course he doesn't like it, because it was my idea. Now are you going to listen to me or to some scrambled egg?"

"You will show some respect," said Winkie.

"There's only one person here worthy of any amount of respect," said Krool. "And that is Elspeth Pule. I threw her down a well, and she came out kicking and screaming. That is deserving of a certain amount of reverence. The rest of you, on the other hand, are a bunch of pathetic losers. Look at you." Krool leveled his gaze at Winkie. "The only reason you're king is because you were born into it. You've done nothing to deserve such privilege."

Winkie, at that moment, wanted nothing more than to put Krool in his place, but he simply could not think of a fitting response. Instead he bit his lip and leered back at his attacker.

"And you," Krool said, turning to the three brothers. "I've never in my life seen such blubbering from grown men. Sniveling about having to live in a shoe. *Oh, boo-hoo, poor us. We smelled like leather, and everyone laughed at us.* Well, if suffering builds character, then you should thank me for all I've done for you."

"Thank you?" said Maury.

"You're welcome," said Krool.

The three brothers clenched their muscular jaws, and their hands moved to the grips of their swords. Bo-Peep, sensing that Krool was about to talk himself into being sliced to pieces, quickly interjected. "You'd be wise to keep your mouth shut," she said.

"Ha!" Krool replied. "Listen to you. You should be thanking me most of all. If not for me, you'd still be wandering around in a field, learning to yodel and smelling of filthy sheep."

"They were not filthy," said Bo-Peep.

"You're right," said Krool. "They were delicious."

The stick moved so quickly and so fluidly that Krool scarcely had time to flinch before it made contact with the side of his squarish jaw. The impact caused his head to snap to one side. He stumbled back and tumbled over the log upon which he had once sat. With a crunch and a thud, he fell into the brush where he lay flat on his back, his legs in the air.

"A little help would be nice." He wheezed as he reached out and found, not a helping hand, but the end of the very stick that had knocked him silly. He grabbed hold of it, and Bo-Peep pulled him up over the log and to his feet. He quickly fell back onto the log and almost off the other side again before regaining his balance. "Well, I suppose I deserved that," he said, blinking excessively and waggling his jaw back and forth.

When his eyes came into focus once more he saw Dumpty standing before him with a wry grin. "Well then," said Dumpty. "Looks like you and I have something in common, old boy. Both prone to bouts of dizziness. Now, shall we get moving, or will I have to roll you the rest of the way?"

Krool asked for and was granted another minute and soon they were on their way again. But not for long. As they approached the cliffs above Torcano Alley, by now the sun had vanished behind the forest in the distance, leaving the sky streaked in purple and pink. Or, if you prefer, dusty rose. Crossing the alley in darkness would be foolish, so they decided to make camp for the night in the soft grass surrounding the oak tree named Beatrice.

None of them relished the idea of camping out in the open while an evil witch of unknown abilities might very well be lurking nearby. Elspeth laid out her bedroll while the three brothers gathered armfuls of dead sticks and twigs to build a fire, an act that Gene found highly objectionable.

"I can't believe this," he moaned as the dry wood crackled in the quivering flames. "Is that any way to show respect for the dead?"

"Actually," said Dumpty, "it's the ultimate show of respect, if you happen to be a Viking."

"A Viking," Gene pondered. "Well, I guess if it was good enough for the Vikings, it's good enough for sticks."

With the camp set and the fire roaring with the souls of Viking sticks, rising upward in the form of bright-orange sparks, the travelers all gathered around for warmth and for what little protection the fire might provide. By now a full moon shone down, gently caressed by slow-moving wisps of cloud in an otherwise clear night sky.

"I suppose I don't need to remind any of you that we will soon be face to face with the epitome of evil," said Winkie, the firelight giving a strange and eerie movement to his face. "I know you're all frightened, and I would just like to say—"

"Is this the one about the guy with the hook for a hand?" asked Gene.

"The what?"

"The ghost story. About the guy with the bloody hook? Or is it the one about the guy who gets buried alive and he has to—"

"This is not a ghost story," Winkie snapped. "We're not here to roast marshmallows and sing folk songs around the campfire. Like it or not, this is real life. And we very well might be facing the end of it. So at this time I would like to offer you all the opportunity to turn back, without shame or judgment."

Winkie scanned the faces around him, and his eyes landed on Elspeth's. "You're but a child," he said. "I was wrong to bring you into this. You should be home with your parents."

Elspeth couldn't have agreed more with this statement. She should have been home with her parents. "You're right. This whole situation is ridiculous and I'm out of here," she said in her head. But those were not the words that came out of her mouth, for she was a hero with a bronze statue standing twelve feet tall in the middle of the castle courtyard. And that is not the sort of thing that heroes say, so instead she replied, "I don't care. I'm going with you. As a natural-born citizen of New Winkieland, Farrah is my queen too. And I'm going to help rescue her."

Winkie only nodded in reply before rising to his feet. He puffed up his cheeks and expelled the air loudly. "All right then. We should probably try and get some sleep."

"Wait a minute," said Gene. "What about him?" He was looking at Krool, and now the others were as well.

"What *about* him?" asked Winkie.

"How do we know he's not going to wait until we all doze off then kill us in our sleep?"

"Good point," said Bo-Peep. "We should take turns standing guard."

"We'll do it," said Rory.

169

At this Krool just chuckled. "Silly people," he said. "The very idea that I would ever kill someone in their sleep. After all, seeing their reaction is half the fun. Besides, I can't take on Mary Mary by myself. So, as hard as it may be for your tiny brains to comprehend and as difficult as it is for me to admit, I need you almost as much as you need me. So the idea of me killing any of you in your sleep is utterly ridiculous. Got it?"

They stared at Krool for a time, and finally Cory said, "I'll take the first shift."

Now I lay me down to sleep,
I pray that I won't dream of sheep.
If I should die before I wake,
Then this was all one big mistake.

Chapter 16

Elspeth suffered nothing in the way of bad dreams that night, simply because in order to dream you must first sleep, something she did very little of between the time they all bedded down and that moment when finally the sun circled around behind them and lightened the sky once more. Only then, when the others were just beginning to stir, did she finally allow herself to slip away.

It may have been an hour but it seemed like only minutes when she woke to a gentle nudging. She looked up to see Bo-Peep's smiling face, speckled with early morning sunshine and shadow from the low-hanging leaves of Beatrice, the great oak.

"Sorry to wake you," said Bo-Peep. "But King William is quite anxious to get going."

"Yes, of course," said Elspeth. With her thumb she pushed some dried gunk from the corners of her eyes and, sitting up, she was instantly aware that her hair was sticking up in several places and at odd angles. It reminded her of Mary Mary with her twisted, knotted hair and acid-filled eyes. While trying unsuccessfully to push down the cowlicks, she looked around and found that everyone else was more or less packed up and ready to go. Winkie was just finishing loading his tiny bedroll onto his armadillo while Dumpty kicked dirt onto what remained of the fire.

Krool, the side of his face marked with a bruise of purple and greenish gold, stood, impatiently fidgeting, while Cory, Rory, and Maury, with no weights to lift, took turns bench-pressing one another.

"Come on, five more!" yelled Cory as Rory lay on his back, grunting and straining to hoist up Maury the suggested number of times. "Feel the burn!"

"Feel the burn?" said Krool, rolling his eyes. "Seriously?"

"So then, we're all still alive," said Elspeth, taking a visual inventory of the group.

"Alive and kicking it," said Gene. "By the way, I love what you've done with your hair."

Elspeth glared down at the stick, lying on the grass next to her.

"What?" he said. "I was only joking."

Elspeth responded by quickly springing to her feet, picking up Gene, and raising her arm into a throwing position. "Wait!" Gene screamed. "No! Don't throw me into the bushes! Please!"

Elspeth lowered her arm and looked at the stick. "What?" She shrugged. "I was only joking."

Gene made no further attempts at humor as Elspeth packed up her bedroll and tried once more with her hair before giving up. Heroes didn't have time to worry about how their hair looked. After all, that's probably why George Washington wore a wig.

"How are you feeling this morning?" she asked as she approached Dumpty, who was busy smacking the dust from the same shoes he'd used to kick dirt onto the fire.

"My vertigo is just fine." He coughed. "My pride, on the other hand . . ."

"Oh, don't be silly," said Elspeth. "No one thinks any less of you for it. According to Krool, a strength can become a weakness. And I think he's right about that. But a weakness can also end up making you stronger, if you're able to overcome it."

Dumpty's scarred face softened, and for the moment he forgot all about his dusty shoes. "How is it that someone so young could be filled with so much wisdom?" he said.

"Pfft," said Elspeth with a dismissive wave of her

hand. "I think I probably read that on one of those cat posters. Anyway, you should be proud that you've never let this thing stop you from doing what you've had to do."

"Thank you," said Dumpty. "I appreciate that."

"Okay," said Winkie, smacking his hands together with purpose. He tightened the armadillo's saddle then climbed upon its back. "Let's get moving here."

"Pardon me," said Dumpty, "but before we continue on, don't you think we should first formulate some kind of a plan?"

"Well, I hate to admit it, but I thought Krool's idea made a great deal of sense," said Winkie. "Entice the witch with the promise of power."

"Begging Your Majesty's pardon," said Dumpty. "But I'm afraid the entire matter is not quite so simple. We face several problems as I see it. First of all, as a mog, Mary Mary may appear to us as any number of animals, people, or . . . meteorological phenomena. We also have no idea as to where she lives other than somewhere in the Thick, which covers no small amount of jungle."

"The smell," offered Elspeth. "Did you notice it? When she appeared as a torcano. The odor was quite strong. Like charcoal."

"I did notice that," Bo-Peep confirmed.

"Yes, I suppose that might be one way to find her," said Winkie.

"In that case I should lead the way," Gene volunteered. "After all, I have a very keen sense of smell. In fact, I'm picking up something right now."

"Sorry," said the armadillo. "That was me. I think I ate a stink bug."

"But what happens if and when we do find her?" asked Bo-Peep. "With the powers she possesses she could easily destroy us all."

Elspeth thought for a moment. "As I understand it, she gets that power from the golden pear. So all we have to do is take it from her."

"And how do you suggest we do that?" asked Winkie.

When Elspeth failed to answer right away, Krool took the opportunity to chime in. "May I?" he said.

"Sure." Winkie sighed. "We'd love to hear what is undoubtedly a brilliant idea."

"Brilliant in its obviousness," said Krool. "In fact, as dim as you all might be, I'm surprised none of you thought of it. That's what happens when you're too nice. It clouds your judgment."

"Just tell us the idea, would you?" said Elspeth with a huff.

"Having been witness to more than my share of executions," said Krool, "there's one thing I've noticed and that is that one's head seems to be very instrumental in keeping a necklace from falling off." Krool turned to the three brothers. "And that's where you boys would come in."

Cory looked at Winkie then back at Krool. "Wait a minute. Are you suggesting we chop off her head?"

"Those swords of yours aren't just for shaving your legs, are they?" Krool sneered. "Of course I'm suggesting you chop off her head. Can you think of a better way to put her out of our misery? To get your queen and my money back?"

The brothers exchanged uneasy glances among themselves. In their limited time in the service of the king, they had never once had to bloody their swords, much less chop someone's head off. Beyond the grisly nature of such an endeavor, there was the issue of proximity. In order to chop off a witch's head, you needed to be in her general vicinity, and the idea of being that close to Mary Mary held little appeal for the boys.

"Sometimes you have to get your hands a little dirty in order to accomplish your objectives," said Krool. "Well then. Now that we have a plan in place, what exactly are we waiting for?" With that, Krool turned and started down the switchback trail, leaving the others standing in silence.

"So?" said Winkie at last. "Is that it then? Our plan is find Mary Mary and chop her head off?"

"If I think of a better one, I'll let you know," said Elspeth.

Winkie sighed, and then he took a quick moment to thank Beatrice for the use of her personal space.

"No worries," she said. "And be sure to say hello to Manuel on your way to the Thick."

"We will indeed," said Winkie.

177

The group formed a single file and followed Krool down into Torcano Alley on their way to find the evil witch and relieve her of the golden pear. And, in the process, her head.

A low fog clung to the ground and shrouded the jungle floor in a thick powder gray. The trees that rose out of the mist were gnarled and pitted, with irregular branches, roped with broad, spiraling vines. The ground from which the roots of the trees nursed was barely solid, covered in loose mud and slippery swamp moss. Even on the brightest of days, the Thick was a world of constant darkness and perpetual gloom.

There was one tree more contorted than its neighbors, as if it had grown that way on purpose in order to accommodate the small shack that sat upon the platform built at the very top of it, among the most deformed of its branches.

The hastily and poorly built shack, like the tree that hosted it, was carpeted with moss and striped with creeping vines. A dim lamplight glowed in the sole window, a glassless, rectangular opening no more than a half foot high and ten inches across.

If one were both brave and foolish enough to climb that tree, branch to crooked branch, and stand upon that creaky platform and stretch up onto tiptoes and peer into the window, his eyes would have met with a most troubling sight. The single room was beset with litter and covered in filth. On the table and on the floor, wriggling maggots feasted on scraps of food, discarded and left to rot. Mold coated the walls in a blackish green, and the exposed rafters were heavy with the webs of large, quick-moving spiders.

A stained and ragged mattress lay on the floor in one corner. Upon that mattress sat a large burlap sack. Spilling forth from it were glass jars full of one-hundred-sixpence notes.

Across the room, tucked away in the shadows of the far corner, was a small cage, perhaps two feet high. Made of sticks tied together with strong, woody vines, the cage, like the shack itself, seemed to be constructed with little know-how. Lying on the floor of the cage, on her side, curled up in a desperate effort to conserve body heat, was Queen Farrah.

Her face shone gaunt and waxen through the tight slots between the sticks. Lack of sleep and food had greatly affected her ability to control her thoughts and had lessened her capacity to cling to any sense of hope. Still, her eyes never left the tiny window as she waited, hour after hour, day after day, for the appearance of a familiar face. And then a face did appear, so suddenly that it caused Farrah to sit up quickly. It was the first time she'd moved since morning. She lurched not forward in anticipation but to the far end of the cage in retreat.

The face, its black eyes reflecting the light from the lamp, searched the room fervently, though quite in vain, for a Germese Stranglerat is far too large to fit through such a tiny opening.

This did not stop the animal from staring hungrily at the cage across the room. Outside the shack, its claws scratched at the wood and its long and powerful tail whipped about wildly, as if overdue for and in desperate need of a good strangling.

And as its nails scratched and its tail quivered, its nostrils began to twitch as well when hit with a new and alarming odor. As quickly and as silently as it had appeared, the stranglerat was gone, scampering quickly down the tree trunk and off in the opposite direction of the stench of burned charcoal and the crimson steam that left a trail through the fog as it moved across the jungle floor toward the shack.

The witch emerged from the gray, floating just above the boggy earth. Only mildly affected by gravity, her gnarled hands and feet propelled her quickly and effortlessly up the trunk of the tree.

Farrah's tiny body stiffened and surged with adrenaline as the door to the shack burst open. Through the bars she could see the witch's chalky eyes, bathed in an orange glow from the lighted lamp and dripping pale-yellow acid onto the floor.

She carried, tucked beneath her right arm, a bundle of sticks. With her foot, she kicked the door, slamming it closed as forcefully as she had opened it, then walked slowly and deliberately toward the cage and dropped the bundle of sticks with a clatter.

She leaned forward and gave the cage a sharp kick and peered in through the top. Acid sizzled as several drops hit the cage and seeped in through the cracks, landing very close to where Farrah sat.

"Well," said Mary Mary. "You're still alive." Her voice was not at all what you might expect from someone so monstrous. It was deep and resonant but smooth and clear—not the raspy, cackling tone normally associated with witches. Furthermore, it sounded less like a person talking and more like the voice of someone deep down in her belly who had been swallowed whole.

"I may not be alive for long if you don't let me go," said Farrah.

"And why would I do that?"

Mary Mary exhaled a reddish puff of air and sat down next to the cage. She picked up two of the sticks she had dropped and, with some strips of vine, began lashing them together.

"Because you got what you wanted," said Farrah. She pulled herself to her feet and moved her face close to the bars. "You got the money. I'm of no use to you now."

"If that were true," said the witch in her smooth,

hollow voice, "then you would no longer be alive. The day you become of no use to me will be your last."

"Then what is it?" Farrah pleaded. "What more do you want?"

"I don't know," said the witch. She took another stick and began connecting it to the first two. "Attention, I suppose."

"Wait a minute," said Farrah. "You mean, you're doing all this just to get attention?"

"You say it as though it's a minor thing," said the witch. She stood again and walked to the fireplace. There she picked up a log from a small woodpile on the hearth and tossed it in. "I will tell you that attention is every bit as vital as food and shelter and warmth." She aimed an index finger at the log. A white light shot forth, instantly setting fire to it. She returned to where she had sat before and went to work once more on attaching another stick to what was starting to look more and more like the beginnings of a tiny wall.

"But just think of the attention you'd get if you returned me safely to the castle," Farrah said. "Why, there would be a parade in your honor and a statue in the courtyard."

The witch looked quickly in Farrah's direction and hissed out a bloodred cloud. "Let me tell you what I don't like," she said. "I don't like being spoken to as if I'm an idiot. Statues and parades are for the beautiful and the noble. Look at me. Look at me!"

Farrah fought to keep her gaze on the witch's white, seeping eyes.

"Have you ever seen a statue that looked like this? Have you?"

"That doesn't mean there couldn't be one."

Mary Mary scoffed at this, then held up the grouping of sticks for inspection. "His and hers cages," she said. "So romantic. They should be here soon. That is, if the beasts don't get them first."

By then, Elspeth and the others had been slogging through the Thick for several hours. With Gene's acute sense of smell, he and Elspeth had taken point with Dumpty and Bo-Peep following closely behind. After that came Krool then the three brothers with Winkie now riding upon Cory's right shoulder. The armadillo had been released into the wild long before they'd entered the forest, and for Winkie to try and walk on his own, the mud would have been up his waist.

"I don't believe this," Krool grumbled as the ground became gloppier with each step forward. "You mean to tell me that nobody thought to bring along a map of this place?"

"I told you, a map to this place doesn't exist," said Dumpty. "So far, no one has had the guts to try and make one, so I'm afraid this remains uncharted territory."

Just then a light breeze shifted and brought with it something to Gene's newly twitching nostrils. Elspeth noticed and quickly held up a hand as a way of calling for quiet. "What is it, Gene?"

Gene closed his eyes and inhaled deeply. "Charcoal," he said.

"Okay," said Elspeth. "I think we should—"

"And passion fruit," Gene continued. "With a soupçon of wild honeysuckle and just a . . . hint of sweaty gym sock."

"I don't care about any of that nonsense," said Elspeth. "Just tell me about the charcoal."

"It's coming from that direction," said Gene.

The sudden realization that they were close to Mary Mary was seen as equal parts triumph and catastrophe. This is what they'd been searching for, but was it really what they wanted to find?

"I suggest we end all verbal communication until further notice," said Elspeth. "The longer our presence is unknown to Mary Mary the better."

"Agreed," said Winkie. "No talking."

"That means you," Elspeth said, staring crossly at Gene. "No talking."

"Okay," said Gene. "You don't have to tell me twice."

"No talking," said Elspeth for the second time.

With a deep breath Elspeth sampled the air, and she could smell it too. She signaled silently with her hand and the group followed her off the path, wading through the tangled brush. The three brothers' swords would have been useful here, though hacking one's way through the undergrowth is not a particularly quiet way to go so the weapons remained sheathed.

By now the scent of charcoal was no longer faint but strong and biting. It seemed that Mary Mary must be very close by, yet they could see no sign of her. Elspeth stopped at the base of a particularly crooked tree. Gene sniffed the air silently while the others watched and waited for further instructions.

"Okay," Gene blurted out suddenly. "Now I'm getting charcoal and garbage."

"Shh!" said Elspeth, clamping her hand over Gene's mouth.

But it was too late. From high atop the tree came the sound of a wooden door on rusty hinges being violently thrown open. Looking up toward the noise, they noticed, for the first time, the old shack upon the platform. Also standing on that platform was Mary Mary, gazing out across the Thick with those soulless white eyes. Elspeth and the others stood nearly motionless. The three brothers placed their hands upon the grips of their swords as the witch parted her shriveled black lips and hissed out a small, bloodred cloud.

Rings around those ghostly
Eye sockets full of mostly
Acid, acid, please don't look down.

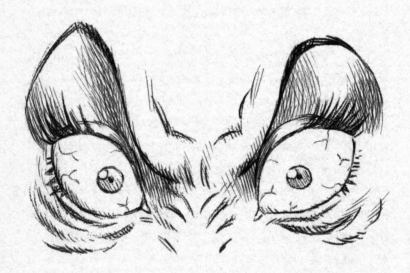

Chapter
17

Silently and breathlessly they huddled as close to the trunk of the tree as possible while squatting down, dipping low into the cover of the fog and ferns. Peering out from behind the leaves they could see the witch, pacing about the platform like a prowling cat. Her clouded eyes scanned the perimeter of the jungle, searching for the source of a sound she wasn't quite sure she had actually heard.

Several drops of acid fell from her eyes over the edge of the platform, and they hit the surrounding plants with a burning hiss. Luckily for those hiding below, Mary Mary's eyesight was not terribly sharp. In the end, the witch decided the noise had been the result of her imagination, and she stormed back into the shack, slamming the door behind her.

Elspeth and the others exhaled slowly, relieved as one might be who has come within inches of the hornet's nest without actually stepping in it. Dumpty's eyes met Elspeth's, and she turned her head sharply away from the tree as if to say, "Let's get out of here."

Dumpty nodded in agreement, and Elspeth led the way, inching as quietly as possible back in the direction they'd come. Only when they had reached the path and decided they had put sufficient distance between the witch and themselves, did anyone dare to speak.

"Well, that was awfully close," whispered Winkie from his perch upon Cory's shoulder.

"Yes," said Dumpty. "That could have gone badly for us. The question is, now what? How do we go about the business of chopping off her head?"

It might have seemed logical that attention would go to Bo-Peep as King William's chief military advisor or to Dumpty as his Minister of Intelligence. Instead, all eyes turned to Lady Elspeth the Conqueror, Duchess of the Deadlands, regional junior chess champion, and master strategist.

Elspeth gnawed at her lower lip as she often did when locked in a fierce chess battle. Other than that, the similarities between chess and her current situation were few. Certainly the goal of each was to make sure the pieces were all positioned for success. And though she'd lost plenty of matches in her career, she'd never been blasted with a bolt of lightning or turned into a muskrat as a result.

But heroes did not beg off when faced with challenges, and as much as she would have loved to defer to one of the others, she did not.

"First of all," she said, "we have to lure her out of that shack and into a trap. And for that, we'll need bait."

"Fine," said Winkie. "What did you have in mind? Food?"

"What I had in mind," said Elspeth, "is you."

"What?" gasped Dumpty. "You're suggesting we use the king as bait?"

"It's okay," said Winkie. "If it'll get Farrah back, I'm happy to be the one to draw Mary Mary into the snare. Go on, Elspeth."

"Sometimes the best traps are the simple ones," said Elspeth. "First, you need to get her attention. Tell her you've got something invaluable to offer. Like Krool said, entice her with the promise of unbridled power. A seat upon the throne."

"And once she's out of the shack?" said Dumpty. "How then do we manage to chop her head off without being turned to ashes, or into pink armadillos?"

"I'm thinking a four-pronged assault is the way to go," said Elspeth, taking a knee on the soggy path. She plunged Gene into the mud to a depth that he could stand on his own.

"Hey," Gene protested. "What's the deal?"

Elspeth ignored Gene and continued. "Let's say Gene is the tree."

"Let's say I'm the stick who does not appreciate being shoved into the mud," said Gene.

"Would you prefer I stuck you in headfirst?" snapped Elspeth.

"Okay," said Gene. "Let's say I'm the tree."

"Good," said Elspeth, who then plucked a few small rocks from beneath a bush and placed one of them a few inches from Gene. "I noticed a log several feet from the tree. King William will position himself upon it here."

She placed another rock behind Gene and one each to the left and to the right of the rock representing Winkie. "Rory, Cory, and Maury," she said. "One of you behind the tree, the others hiding in the bushes here and here, with your swords drawn, ready to attack."

"That's three prongs," said Bo-Peep. "May I assume I'm the fourth?"

"You'll be here," said Elspeth, placing a rock behind Winkie's. "Lying alongside the log. If King William can entice her here, she'll end up in zugzwang."

"Zugzwang," said Gene. "What is that, a type of sausage?"

"It's a chess term," said Elspeth. "It means that any move she makes will weaken her position. When I give the signal, the first thing we'll do is a bit of castling. King William will drop down behind the log while Bo-Peep, our trusty rook, leaps up and charges forward. With Mary Mary's focus on her, the brothers will move in for the kill."

When she looked at Cory, Rory, and Maury, she was hoping not to see such looks of uncertainty.

"What if we miss?" asked Cory.

"Don't," said Elspeth. "And remember. You can do this."

While Rory and Cory looked hesitant yet resigned, Maury, the youngest of the three, was suddenly a trembling mess. "I-I can't," he stammered. "I'm sorry, but I just can't do it." He sat on a log and buried his face in his sweaty palms.

"Fine," said Krool. "I would be delighted to take your place." He extended his open hand and Maury could only stare at it.

"If you think we're going to give you a sword, you're crazy," said Winkie.

"You'd be crazy not to," said Krool. "I'm quite handy with one, I assure you. And when I've finished with it you have my word as a gentleman that I shall return it as good as new, though perhaps a bit on the messy side. Well? What do you say?"

Winkie looked for Elspeth for guidance.

"Give him the sword," she instructed Maury.

The young man sighed and made no effort to hide his shame as he stood and unbuckled his belt and handed it over, sword and all. Not nearly as fit as Maury, Krool was forced to expand the belt by a couple of notches before it would rest comfortably around his middle.

"Okay," said Elspeth. "Remember, when you attack, do it quickly. Even the slightest hesitation could be the death of us all."

Elspeth reached into her jacket pocket, removed her set of apartment keys, and handed them to Winkie.

"What's this?"

"The keys to the kingdom."

At the very moment that Elspeth handed those keys to Winkie, back in Banbury Cross, Jill was fishing her own house keys from her pocket as she made her way up the walk after a long day at work. She entered the tiny cottage and instantly found the quiet inside troubling. As a garbage collector, Jack always finished his work earlier and, without fail, met his wife at the door with a kiss and a freshly brewed cup of tea.

"Jack?" she called out. When her voice was met with silence, she walked first to the bedroom and poked her head in, only to find it every bit as unpopulated as the living room. Resigned to making her own tea this day, she walked to the kitchen and that's where she saw the note, folded in half and propped up like a pup tent upon the countertop. Slowly, she opened the note and read.

"My deerest wife," began the message, written by a man with a fourth-grade education. "I'm sory I had to do this to you, but reguardless of my own sircumstances, I'm just not abel to sit around and do nothing while Elspeth may be in grave danger. I'll be back as soon as I can. Your loving husband, Jack."

Jill wasted only a few short moments staring out the kitchen window before silently cursing her husband, then hurrying out of the house, up the hill on her way to the castle.

One might think that as the mother of a local hero-ine, Jill would be granted unlimited access to the royal palace, but this was not the case. She, like everyone not officially within the king's inner circle, was stopped cold at the gate.

"Pardon me," she said to the sentries flanking the entryway on either side. "I'm Jill Jillson."

"Yes," said the guard on the right, in the same tone that one would say, "And?"

"Elspeth Pule's mother," Jill clarified.

"I know who you are," said the guard, a man with a startling lack of facial expression. "What do you want?"

"Please," she begged. "I must see Sir Fergus immediately."

"And to what is it pertaining?" replied the guard on the left, a thin, dark man with a short, choppy way of speaking.

"I can't say," Jill stammered in return.

"Then I can't let you in," said the guard.

"But it's a matter of great importance."

"Sir Fergus is a very busy owl," said the guard on the right. "Everything he does is of great importance."

Jill might have given up right there if Georgie, on his way to the village to purchase a belated wedding gift for the Dish and the Spoon, hadn't walked out of the castle courtyard and across the drawbridge at that very moment.

"Georgie," Jill said, taking him by the forearm. "You've got to help me."

"But of course, Jill," Georgie replied. "Anything. What is it?"

"I need to speak to Sir Fergus right away."

Georgie immediately decided that purchasing monogrammed dish towels for the newlyweds could wait until later, and he personally escorted Jill into the castle and through the narrow halls to the office of Sir Fergus, which looked far more like a library than anything else. Floor-to-ceiling bookshelves covered two walls, and several stacks of books sat upon the large wooden desk. Fergus stood on the desk amid the books as he finished dictating a letter to his personal assistant, a stout, red-bearded Welshman by the name of Taffy, who sat in a chair, trying to scribble every bit as fast as Fergus could speak.

"And furthermore," Fergus intoned with a sense of

great indignation, "may I remind you, Mr. Chairman, that the scientific community is in clear agreement that there is no basis for the assertion that little boys are made of snips and snails and puppy dog tails and that little girls are made of sugar and spice and everything nice. As such, I respectfully decline your request that such teachings be added to the biology curriculum of the Banbury Cross public school system. Sincerely, Sir Fergus, Minister of Education." He waited for Taffy to catch up before adding, "Now read that back to me, please."

Taffy placed a fist over his bearded mouth and cleared his throat, then read it back. Fergus wasn't sure. "Too nice, I think. Don't you?"

"Agreed," said Taffy. "Too nice, considering."

"Why do these lunatics insist upon teaching our children these ridiculous fairy tales?" said Fergus.

Before Taffy could answer, the door to the office opened just enough to allow Georgie's head to poke in. "Sorry to bother you, Sir Fergus," he said. "Jill Jillson is here to see you. She says it's a matter of great importance."

"Well, by all means, send her in," Fergus replied.

Georgie swung the door aside, and Jill entered the room with purpose. "Jill," said Fergus at the sight of her. "I heard the horrible news. Let me say that I have no doubt that Jack is fully innocent of the charges leveled against him."

"Thank you," said Jill. "It's been quite an ordeal."

"Tell me," said Fergus. "What can I do for you?"

Jill looked at Taffy, and then at Georgie with hesitance.

Fergus immediately picked up on her discomfort. "Gentlemen," he said. "If you wouldn't mind."

"Not at all, sir," said Taffy and he and Georgie quickly and quietly left the room, closing the door behind them.

"What is it, Jill?" asked Fergus, keeping his voice low. "What's on your mind?"

"It's Jack," she replied. "He's jumped bail."

"Jumped bail?"

"He's gone off to the Thick to find Elspeth."

"Oh dear," said Fergus. "You do realize that if this gets out they'll send the bounty hunters after him. Good gracious, what was he thinking?"

"He wasn't, I'm afraid," said Jill. "Truth is, he's been sick with guilt and worry since she left."

Fergus nodded thoughtfully. "I've been quite worried myself, so I can only imagine what it must be like as the girl's parent. So, tell me. What can I do to help you?"

Jill walked to the window and looked down into the courtyard at the statue of Elspeth. "Stress and worry have clouded his thinking. I'm afraid it'll cause him to get careless. I would go after him if I could, but he's got a half-day's head start on me. I was just thinking that if someone—"

"Yes, I see," said Fergus. "I'll do it. I'll go after him."

"Thank you," said Jill, her shoulders slumping in sudden relief. "I'm sorry to trouble you, with your injury and all. I would ask someone else, but there's no one I trust."

"Shh," said Fergus, raising a single feather to his beak. "Not another word about it. I will find your husband. But if I know him as I do, convincing him to turn around and come back will be another matter altogether."

Jack be troubled,
Jack be sick,
Jack jumped bail
and ran off to the Thick.

Chapter
18

Mary Mary held up the completed first wall of the new cage and admired her handiwork. In fact, she was so pleased with herself that she might not have noticed the tiny voice calling her name at all if Farrah hadn't sat up suddenly and gasped, "William!"

The witch turned her ear toward the open window, and there it was again, faint but insistent. Her black lips curled into something resembling a smile. "He's come for you," she said. "And sooner than I thought. You may have to share a cage for the first day or two until I can finish my work." She set the sticks aside, stood, and walked to the door.

With her limited eyesight, it took a moment for Mary Mary to pick Winkie out of the landscape. When she finally saw him standing on that log, shouting her name, she grinned and let out a breath that smelled and looked like smoke and fire.

From her position upon a nearby hill, with Gene in her hand and Dumpty at her side, Elspeth crouched and peered through the leaves of the ground cover at the witch in her vaulted position. At Elspeth's other side was Maury, humiliated yet thankful to have been relieved of duty.

Hiding in their assigned spots, Cory, Rory, and Krool held tightly to their swords and Bo-Peep lay motionless behind the log as Winkie shouted, "I have a proposal I think you will find most interesting."

"Your friends," said the witch, slowly surveying the area. "What's become of them?"

"They've abandoned me," said Winkie, doing a poor job of selling it. Elspeth thought the king could desperately use some acting lessons. "Cowards, the lot of them."

The witch took a moment to decide whether she believed King William. At the end of it, she still wasn't sure, though it didn't seem to matter that much to her either way. "You said something about a proposal," she shouted down.

"Yes," said Winkie. "But first I must know that the queen is alive and well."

"She is," said Mary Mary, leaving Winkie desperate for more.

"Forgive my cynicism, but I would like visual proof of that," he said, trying to strike a tone that was both assertive and deferential.

Should she be agreeable or not? Mary Mary seemed to consider these two options before finally turning and walking back into the shack while Winkie tried very hard to keep from hyperventilating. A moment later, the witch reappeared, holding the tiny cage.

"Farrah!" Winkie cried. And though at this distance and with the spaces between the wooden bars being so narrow, he could not actually see the queen, he knew in his heart she must be inside it. And when she slipped a slender arm between the bars, reaching in vain for her husband, and simply uttered his name, the king felt as though his heart might burst. "Are you okay, my dear?"

"I'm okay," came the voice, weaker than Winkie had ever known it.

"So?" said the witch. "What am I bid for this lovely specimen?"

"Everything," said Winkie.

"Everything?"

From behind his back, Winkie produced the set of keys. "The kingdom. It's all yours if you will only let her go."

The witch looked at the keys then at the cage and thought that such a lopsided exchange must surely come with some kind of a catch. The very idea that someone would give up his entire kingdom to save the life of one person, beloved wife or otherwise, seemed ludicrous.

"And I would be queen?" the witch asked skeptically.

"You would be queen," Winkie confirmed.

"And all would bow down before me?"

"If you so command them."

"Well, of course I would," said the witch. "What's the point of lording over others if you can't make them worship you?"

Mary Mary had no way of knowing that she was speaking to a man who was, despite his tiny stature, above such things. In all his years upon the throne, Winkie had never had any desire to be worshiped, praised, or venerated in any way. And while forcing others to grovel at one's feet held no interest for most, to others, like Krool and Mary Mary, such a thing was pure catnip.

"I agree," said Winkie, his acting skills having improved a little over the last few exchanges. "There's nothing quite like being worshiped. You're going to love it."

"There will be a ceremony," said the witch. "A coronation, in which you will place the crown upon my head and declare me ruler of the land of Mary-Maryville."

Just as Winkie allowed himself to think that the witch had fallen for the scheme, Farrah shouted, "William, you mustn't."

The witch glared at the cage and for a moment seemed to be on the verge of tossing it from the platform to the ground, too far below for Farrah to survive such a fall.

"Keep quiet in there," she said. "You can choose to be a live peasant or a dead queen."

"Please, Farrah," said Winkie. "Say no more. I happily give up the throne for your safety."

"But the people. You can't do this to the people."

Winkie began to panic. He hadn't counted on this. If the witch's vision were better, she would have noticed Winkie's eyes moving up to the hill where Elspeth hid. Elspeth glared urgently from behind the leaves, and the king's eyes moved back to the cage.

"We will make the exchange now," he said.

"Very well," said Mary Mary. "But do not forget that I command the beasts of the Thick. To double-cross me would result in both you and your bride being torn to shreds by the likes of the Great Spiny Gleekin."

"I understand," said Winkie. "Now let's get on with it."

As the witch, with cage in hand, began to slowly descend from the tree, Cory removed his hand from his sword just long enough to wipe his sweaty palm on the leg of his pants.

Elspeth watched intently, gauging and scrutinizing the witch's every move. To give the order to attack too soon or too late could bear very bad results.

Mary Mary now stood at the base of the tree, and for a moment Elspeth thought that maybe she would give the order early after all, with Cory being so very close.

"Toss them here," said the witch.

"No," replied Winkie. "You must bring Farrah to me."

"I think you'd agree that you're in no position to make such demands," said the witch.

"Perhaps not. But I must insist."

The witch took one last look around with her limited vision then walked slowly toward Winkie. The keys jingled like wind chimes as the king's hand began to shake more rapidly with each step the witch took in his direction. When she was just a few feet away, she lowered the cage to the ground, then held out her hand for the keys.

Winkie reached out and leaned forward and the witch did the same. Elspeth inhaled slowly and deeply, and when the witch's fingers touched the trembling keys, Elspeth shouted, "Now!"

Instantly, Winkie dropped down behind the log while Bo-Peep jumped up and charged. The witch's index finger shot out, and from it raced a bolt of white light. The charge, aimed at Bo-Peep's heart, met instead with her wooden staff. Sparks flew as the stick splintered upon impact, the force knocking Bo-Peep to the ground, unarmed and helpless.

The witch lowered her finger and took aim again, but before she could fire, she heard the cracking of a twig and turned to see Rory lumbering toward her from the right, his sword raised high.

As he prepared to bring it around and as the witch leveled her finger at his rapidly beating heart, his foot caught a large root. Down to the slimy ground he fell as a white flare sped from Mary Mary's finger, across the way to the trunk of a tall, thin tree.

The blast snapped the tree in two, its upper half falling toward Cory as he raced up from behind. When the tree knocked him to the ground, Elspeth, Dumpty, and Maury gasped and sprang to their feet. Of their four-pronged attack, there was only one left, and he was nearly upon her.

With muscles flexed and teeth clenched, Krool swung his sword at the witch's neck. The steel sliced first through the air and then through the flesh. The wound spat blood across the swordsman's face and into his eyes. And when he wiped the blood away with the sleeve of his shirt, those very eyes were met with the horrible realization that he had done precisely what Elspeth had told him not to. He had missed.

The witch ran her hand across the superficial wound and inspected the sticky blood. Then she glowered at the man who had tried to chop off her head and raised a bright-red finger in his direction.

"For you," she said, "there will be something far worse than death."

"No," pleaded Krool. "Please."

At the top of the hill, Elspeth, Maury, and Dumpty stood paralyzed in fear. The stress was such that Dumpty's vertigo hit him hard and sudden, leaving Elspeth no chance of catching him before he fell forward and began to roll. All she could do was sprint after him as he bounded down the hill, picking up speed like a dislodged boulder. Dumpty's scream alerted the witch to turn around but not in time to avoid the sprawling half man, half egg.

With considerable force he barreled into the witch, knocking her back and to the ground before continuing on, only stopping when he collided with a large tree.

The witch, stunned and in pain, sought to spring to her feet, but found her bloody neck pinned to the ground by the sole of a muddy shoe. The shoe belonged to Elspeth, who reached down, took hold of the rusted chain around the witch's neck, and pulled sharply until the chain snapped.

With her foot still planted firmly upon the witch's neck, Elspeth raised the glimmering pear high into the air, as if she had just torn Mary Mary's heart from her chest and was putting it on display. And in a way, that's exactly what she had done. With the breaking of the chain came the severing of the witch's ties to her supernatural powers and, as a result, victory.

"Mary Mary," said Elspeth. "You are hereby under arrest for robbery, attempted murder, and the kidnapping of Her Majesty, Queen Farrah."

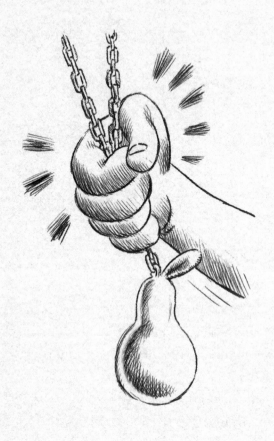

One stunned witch has fallen down,
Fallen down, fallen down.
One stunned witch has fallen down,
It's my pear, lady.

Chapter 19

With his sword, Cory sawed through several of the vines holding the cage together, then peeled the wall back and out climbed Farrah, thin and haggard but relieved and overjoyed. Winkie took her in his arms and gave what seemed to be too forceful a hug to someone so frail.

"I was hoping you'd come," she sobbed. "And I was hoping you wouldn't. She could just as easily have killed you all."

"But she didn't," said Winkie. "And never will she hurt anyone again."

"Thank you," said Farrah.

"You must never leave me," said Winkie. "I fear that I would die without you."

"Then you will live forever," said Farrah. "Because I'm not going anywhere. You have my word on that." She then broke the embrace so she could address the others. Rory and Maury, his sword returned as promised, were standing guard over the witch while Elspeth, Gene, and Bo-Peep tended to Dumpty and his many bumps and bruises. Krool, on the other hand, had only one thing in mind. By then, he was halfway up the tree in search of the stolen money.

"For all you've done I will always be grateful," said the queen. "And I hope one day to find a way to repay you for your bravery and selflessness."

"Long live the queen!" shouted Gene.

"Long live the queen!" echoed the others several times as Winkie pulled Farrah close again. Eager to welcome the queen back herself, Elspeth started over toward Farrah, but Dumpty stopped her with an outstretched arm.

"Maybe give them a moment."

"Sure," said Elspeth. She twirled the golden pear around once before placing it in her jacket pocket, along with her house keys, for safekeeping. As she did, Dumpty suddenly looked unwell and lowered himself to a log. A low moan accompanied the movement.

"Are you sure you're okay?" asked Bo-Peep.

Dumpty waved his hand dismissively. "Ah. No worse than falling off a wall. Just need to sit for a moment." He grimaced then reached around and down the back of his pants. He pulled out a pinecone and tossed it aside.

"And didn't I tell you?" said Elspeth. "That sometimes a weakness can become a strength?"

"What are you on about?" asked Dumpty while removing a twig from his ear.

"Your vertigo. It saved the day. If you hadn't toppled over and rolled down the hill, we'd all be dead."

"Or we'd all be pink armadillos," said Bo-Peep.

"Or dead pink armadillos," said Gene.

"I suppose," said Dumpty. "Still, it would be nice to be able to say that it was by design and not by accident."

"Then that's what we will say," said Bo-Peep.

Dumpty hemmed and hawed. "Well, I don't know if I would feel comfortable saying—"

"Then say what you want," said Elspeth. "But we will say that you threw yourself down the hill to save us all. And that will be the official account."

With the sound of glass jars clinking together, Krool climbed down the tree, the sack slung over his shoulder. With several feet to go, he elected to jump and landed with a crunch on the shrubs below. He walked over to Elspeth and dumped the contents of the bag at her feet. "It's all here," he said. "She didn't spend a single sixpence. Some people just don't know how to live. I mean, at least hire a housekeeper. You should see the inside of that place. Disgusting."

With his foot, Krool separated the jars into two groups of ten. "Well, look at that," he said. "Your king gets his queen *and* he gets to keep the ransom. It's a win-win."

Krool crouched down and went to work opening the jars and removing the notes. "No sense in carrying all these jars around." He stuffed the wads of bills into his pockets and stood once more. "Well then, I guess this is good-bye. It was lovely seeing you again."

"Yeah, it was a real scream," said Elspeth. "And now that you have your money, just don't forget your part of the bargain. You're never to set foot in Banbury Cross again."

"You needn't worry about that," said Krool. "I'm off to far more interesting destinations, I assure you."

"If you make it there," said Elspeth. "Remember, the Thick is crawling with terrible beasts."

"Of which I am one," said Krool. "Don't think that I don't know that." He offered Elspeth his hand. "Best of luck to you."

For a long moment, Elspeth just stared at the very hand that had once dropped her down a well and left her to die. Then she took it. "Same to you," she said. "And by the way, how did you know? About the lambs?"

At this Krool laughed, draped his free arm across Elspeth's shoulders, and gave her a very unwelcome shake and a pat on the back. "Silly girl. It is a fool who believes his dreams are his and his alone," he said. "One day, perhaps you'll know what that means."

Elspeth pulled away from Krool's grasp. "I think it's time for you to leave," she said.

Krool nodded his head briefly. "Very well. Until we meet again." He offered his right hand to Dumpty and to Bo-Peep, and each in turn shook it as a common courtesy—a friendly exchange between sworn enemies allied against another. "It was a pleasure doing business with you," Krool said. "And Dumpty?"

"Yes?"

"You're a good egg."

Krool's smile was not returned by Dumpty, who couldn't be sure whether he was being praised or mocked. Then Krool turned on his heel and walked off into the Thick. And as Elspeth watched him go, she was surprised that she could not find the hatred she'd held for him for so long. Instead, she felt some strange combination of relief and foreboding—a strong sense that the long nightmare had either finally ended or was really just beginning.

Once Krool had vanished among the trees, Elspeth and Bo-Peep went to work removing the money from the jars and stuffing it into Bo-Peep's pockets.

"Hello, Elspeth," said Farrah.

Elspeth looked up to find the queen standing hand in hand with Winkie. Elspeth put her work aside and hugged her friend carefully. "Are you okay? Did she harm you in any way?"

"I'm fine," said Farrah. "Thanks to you."

"Oh, I didn't do anything," said Elspeth. "I was hiding in the bushes while everyone else did all the work.

Bo-Peep attacked the witch head on, and Dumpty here threw himself down the hill like a bowling ball."

"Actually, that's not entirely true," said Dumpty.

"Yes," said Elspeth. "It was more like a cannonball. Anyway, these two and the three brothers over there are your real heroes."

"Agreed," said Winkie. "Their acts were indeed noble. But you rallied us together. With your determination and leadership."

"And your kick-butt attitude," said Gene.

"And, in addition to saving the queen, I see you've recovered the money," said Winkie.

"It's all here," said Bo-Peep. "I'm a bit surprised that Krool didn't try and take more than his share. He was alone with it in the shack, so he certainly could have."

"Hmm," said Winkie. "Not nearly enough to change my opinion of the man."

"Well, he's gone now," said Elspeth. "Now if you don't mind, I'd like to get going. I told Jack and Jill I'd try to stop by for dinner at their place before going home."

"Very well," said Winkie. "Home it is."

Of course Elspeth had no way of knowing that by the time she and the others started out toward Banbury Cross, Jack had managed to limp his way across Torcano Alley and into the forest on the other side.

213

The path he took meandered through the trees and, in time, brought him to the place where Manuel, the grand, sweeping willow, had stood for as many years as his trunk had rings.

"*Hola, Señor* Jack," said Manuel, upon seeing Jack, the limp making him easily identifiable even at a distance.

"Hello, Manuel," said Jack as he lumbered up and gave a hearty handshake to an outstretched branch. "How have you been keeping?"

"Getting old," Manuel replied. "I think I'm losing my bark. And my roots are receding. Oh well. Happens to the best of us. So what brings you to my neck of the woods, *señor*?"

"Looking for Elspeth," said Jack. "You haven't seen her, have you?"

"Indeed," said Manuel. "Twice in the last couple of days. Once going that way, once going this way." He used his branches to point first toward the castle and next toward the Thick.

"When?" asked Jack. "How long ago?"

"Couple of days," said Manuel. "It's a shame about Krool. That they had to let him out of prison."

"She told you about that, did she?"

"Didn't have to," said Manuel. "He was standing right there. So close I could have stuck a twig up his horrible little nose."

"He's still traveling with them?" said Jack. He tried

hard to think of a good reason for such a thing but came up empty. "Why?"

"I don't ask a lot of questions," said Manuel with a shrug of his branches. "It's better that way."

"Yes," Jack agreed. "Sometimes I wish there were things I didn't know. Well then, wish me luck."

"*Vaya con Dios,*" Manuel replied. "Be sure to stop by on your way back."

"You can count on it."

And with that, the willow shook Jack's hand once more and watched as he continued on, deeper and deeper into the forest.

Now there was no clear demarcation between the forest and the Thick. There were no signs indicating where one ended and the other began. It was a change gradual enough that it could catch a person off guard, like a swimmer realizing too late that he'd drifted too far from shore and had been caught up in the pull of the riptide. It was every bit as easy to realize too late that you had left the forest behind and entered the Thick.

And that's exactly what happened to Jack. The first thing he noticed was that his feet did not come up quite so easily from the ground, which had become increasingly moist and sticky. The canopy slowly became denser, and the sunlight from above, more obscured.

The lack of natural light made it difficult to search out footprints that might keep him on the trail of Elspeth's traveling party. Leaning low and forward and brushing ferns and shrubs aside, he studied the ground closely each time he came to a place where the path split into two. So focused was he on looking that he completely forgot to listen, for if he had, he might have noticed the distinct swishing sound that can only be made by the tail of the Germese Stranglerat as it scurries through the undergrowth.

By the time Jack noticed the noise, it was far too late to do much in the way of self-defense. He straightened up and turned just in time to see the massive pink tail slicing through the fog and swinging toward him. It hit him chest high with a sharp slap and wrapped around his middle, pinning his arms to his side. In an instant, the grip tightened, pushing the air from his lungs.

Unable to scream as the tail swung him close to the animal's beady black eyes and long white teeth, Jack could only watch until the lack of oxygen began to blur his vision. And then, with his last bit of reasoning, he opened his mouth, stretched out his neck, and bit the end of the tail.

The stranglerat screeched in agony. Its tail whipped about spasmodically as Jack clenched his jaw with every bit of strength he had left. Finally, the rat's grip loosened and the wild motion of its tail sent Jack flying through the air.

Before he could draw in a much needed breath, he hit

the ground with force and tumbled through the mud and down a steep ravine, over rocks and roots all the way to the bottom where he lay in a patch of thick mud. When he was finally able to inhale, it became instantly apparent that he had broken several if not all of his ribs in the fall. Or perhaps they had been broken by the grip of the stranglerat's powerful tail.

How they'd become cracked was of little consequence. All that mattered now was that he was completely unable to move anything more than his eyes, which were now focused on the top of the hill where the angry stranglerat stared back with hunger in its eyes and gurgling in its stomach.

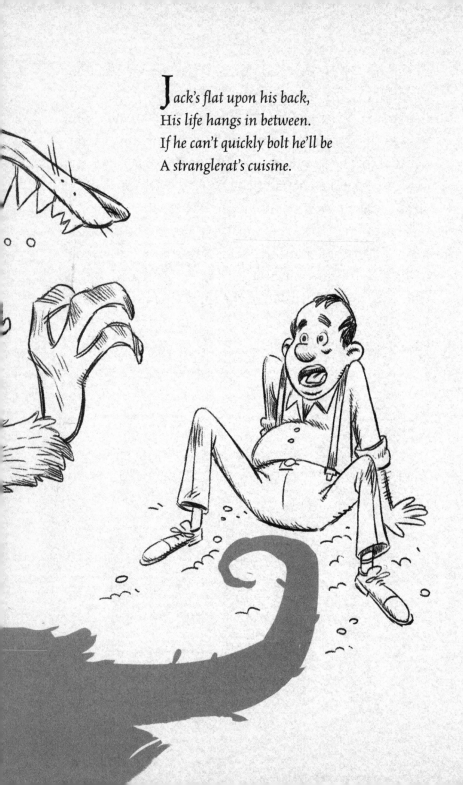

Jack's flat upon his back,
His life hangs in between.
If he can't quickly bolt he'll be
A stranglerat's cuisine.

Chapter 20

The famously sharp, telescopic vision of an owl is surprisingly ineffective when that same owl is soaring above the unchecked growth of the Thick while trying to spot something in the darkness far below it.

Searching only on instinct and on the limited information Manuel was able to provide, Fergus glided just inches above the tops of the deformed and fiendish-looking trees. In just moments it became apparent that to have any chance of finding Jack he would have to dive down, beneath their twisted branches and the cover of their broad leaves. The transition into the Thick may be a gradual one when traveling by foot, but to plummet straight into it from above was to go instantly from day to night.

Fergus's pupils quickly adjusted to the darkness as

his flapping wings propelled him in random directions just above that heavy, loitering fog. Negotiating the labyrinth of thick trunks and contorted branches was made all the more difficult by his complete inability to turn to the right.

In the end, it was this very affliction that led to Jack's discovery. Fergus, forced to circle left in order to turn in the direction he thought he should be going, heard a faint and desperate sound just ahead. Though it was only noise with no words to accompany it, Fergus felt instantly that he knew the source of it.

By the time his eyes landed upon his friend, Jack was still flat on his back at the bottom of the ravine, engaged in a desperate bid to fend off the stranglerat with a large stick, who was none too happy about his inclusion in any of this.

"Put me down," the stick demanded as Jack jabbed it sharply toward the beast. "I don't want to be involved. This is between you and the rat."

But Jack held firmly to the stick and continued to thrust it in the stranglerat's direction as the hungry predator's tail sliced through the air with the sound of a bullwhip.

Without caution or a plan of attack, Fergus let out a screech so fierce it caused the stranglerat to turn quickly away from Jack, just in time to see two fully flexed talons coming toward its puzzled face. Its beady eyes widened, and it let out a squeaky sort of growl.

The owl's claws caught the rat's nose and scratched it badly as Fergus banked sharply away and circled back for a renewed attack. And as the stranglerat shook its head, trying to expel the pain from its bleeding snout, Jack stretched his arm forward, as far as his broken ribs would allow, but still he could not reach the animal's tail. He would have to sit up.

With a good deal of abdomen but little abdominal muscle, Jack would have had a hard time even without a collection of cracked ribs. As it was, he could barely lift his head. The pain nearly caused him to black out as finally he willed himself to a sitting position. He took hold of the tail and quickly tied it around the stick in a tight knot.

"Whoa now," said the stick. "Just what do you think you're doing here?"

Jack did not answer, instead using what little breath he had to let out a groan of agony as he fell back onto his bed of mud.

By now Fergus was again flying directly toward the stranglerat, which remained unaware of the stick tied to its tail and had risen to its hind legs in preparation for battle. The great owl flexed his talons once more and let out a shriek more ghastly than the first. He took another swipe at the creature's face as he flew by, but this time he missed.

Instinctively, the stranglerat whipped its tail at the passing bird. And though the tail soared above the animal's head, the stick did not—instead, sailing directly into its skull. Far more fierce than intelligent, the stranglerat had no idea that he had just clobbered himself in the head, and he spun around, looking for the second attacker.

When Fergus took another pass, again the rat took a swipe and once more the stick connected with the side of its head. Four more times, Fergus circled back and dive-bombed the beast. With each attack, in an attempt to knock the owl from the air with its mighty tail, the stranglerat ended up striking itself in the head until finally it fell in a heap to the muddy, mist-covered ground.

"Fergus," Jack wheezed as the owl circled left and landed very close to the fallen rat. "Is it dead?"

"Nope," said the stick. "I'm fine. Which is pretty amazing considering how many times that thing hit me with its face. Seriously, did you see that?"

"I believe he was referring to the stranglerat," Fergus replied. "And the answer is yes, the wretched thing does appear to have beaten itself to death."

As Fergus started toward Jack, the stick stopped him. "Hold on," it said. "You're not going to leave me tied to this thing, are you? I mean, it's going to start to stink in a couple of days."

"Oh, very well," said Fergus, and with his talons he succeeded in undoing the knot in the dead animal's tail.

"Much better," said the stick as Fergus fluttered over to where Jack lay in the mud.

"Thank goodness you're here," Jack gasped. "That thing was about to make a meal of me."

"Would have served you right," said Fergus. "After all, what kind of fool goes off into the Thick by himself?"

"A heartsick fool," said Jack.

"I understand," said Fergus. "I only wish you'd consulted me beforehand. Tell me, are you able to stand?"

Jack tried to sit up as he had before but this time fell far short of that goal. His painful efforts instantly answered Fergus's question.

"It's my ribs." Jack groaned. He lowered his head to the ground again and stared upward, longing for just a glimpse of blue sky. "I think they're broken."

Fergus nodded slowly then looked worriedly in all directions. There was not much available to the eye that might inspire hope. And then there were those things the eye could not see. Any number of savage creatures might be lurking behind the trees or cloaked in the fog. Still, there was only one thing to be done.

"I'm going to go for help," said Fergus.

"You mean you're going to leave me here? Alone?"

Fergus avoided looking directly at Jack. He knew if he saw the desperation on his friend's face, he might not have the will to leave him behind.

"It's the only way to get you out of here alive," said Fergus. "But you won't be alone."

With two quick flaps of his expansive wings, Fergus was standing near the fallen stranglerat. "You," he said to the stick. "I need you to stay with my friend while I go for help."

Before the stick could confirm or deny his willingness to keep Jack company and provide him with a means of self-defense, Fergus took it in his talons and, a little bit at a time, began dragging it back toward his friend.

"Wait a minute," the stick protested. "You're just going to drag me around like a sack of spuds? Don't I have some say in this? This is ridiculous. It's like my cousin Gene always says, we never get the respect we deserve."

Fergus dropped the stick, then turned and simply stared at it for a moment.

"What?" said the stick. "You don't think we're entitled to a little common courtesy?"

"Did you say you have a cousin named Gene?"

"I did indeed," the stick confirmed. "Little guy. Never shuts up. Why? You know him?"

"Oh, I know him all right," said Fergus.

"You don't say," remarked the stick. "Small world. So tell me, what's old Geno up to these days?"

"If all goes according to plan," said Fergus, "you'll be able to ask him yourself."

Fergus finished the task of dragging the stick close enough to Jack that he could grab hold of it. "Here," he said. "I know it's not much, but this is the best I can do for now."

"Well, way to make a guy feel useful," said the stick.

"Gene's cousin," Fergus explained.

At that moment, Jack couldn't care less whether the stick was a direct descendant of the very first Louisville Slugger. His only interest in it was as a way of protecting himself from further attack during the time it would take Fergus to summon help.

"Okay," said Fergus. "I'll be right back, so don't go anywhere."

"Please," said Jack. "It hurts when I laugh. It also hurts when I talk, breathe, or have to fight off wild animals, so be quick about it, would you?"

"I'll do my best," said Fergus. "And you—stick. Take good care of my friend."

"Kevin," said the stick. "The name is Kevin. Not that you would ever think to ask."

Fergus responded with a shake of his head then took to the air, weaving through the trees and above the fog, keeping his eyes and ears open for any sign of Elspeth and the others. With each minute that passed, his search became increasingly frantic. The Thick covered no small amount of real estate, and certainly more than one owl with a bad wing could be expected to search quickly and efficiently.

He was therefore filled with relief when he heard a familiar voice prattling on about how it was sticks who gave humans the idea to rub two of them together to make a fire. Fergus banked sharply toward the annoying voice, and soon the group came into view.

He flew quickly and unsteadily in their direction, then pulled up, wobbled a bit, and landed at Elspeth's feet, rolling across the ground until Elspeth reached out and stopped his forward momentum.

"Fergus," she said as the bird climbed to his feet and shook the wet soil from his feathers. "What are you doing here?"

"I see you've rescued the queen. That's wonderful news," said Fergus, bowing in Farrah's direction before quickly turning back to Elspeth. "But I'm afraid I bring some that is not so good. It's your father. He needs your help."

"Why? What's happened?"

"He jumped bail and ran off to the Thick to find you."

"Jumped bail? What are you talking about?"

"I'll explain when we get there. We must go at once. He's badly hurt and very vulnerable to a renewed attack. Perhaps a mile from here."

"Renewed attack?" said Elspeth. "He's been attacked?"

"As I said, I'll explain later. This way!"

Without further discussion of the matter, the group followed Fergus as he flew from branch to branch while urging them onward. "Hurry now. There's no time to waste."

It wasn't Elspeth he had to spur onward. Wracked with

worry and plagued by an imagination that flourished in the absence of information, she hurried along the path, wondering in what condition she would find her father. There was no need to prod her. It was another of them slowing things down. Mary Mary had steadfastly refused to quicken her pace, forcing Rory and Maury to drag her along between them.

"Let me go," she snarled, her charcoal breath causing the brothers to choke and gag. "I promise you that one day you will suffer greatly for this."

The boys were pretty sure that that day was now and that they were already suffering by virtue of having to touch such a hideous creature.

"This way," shouted Fergus as he rounded a corner to the left.

Bo-Peep and Dumpty hurried along behind Elspeth. Cory, with the king and queen upon his shoulders, came next, with his witch-dragging brothers trailing the group.

It might have been fifteen or twenty minutes, but to Elspeth it seemed like hours before Fergus said, "He's right up here." He led them off the path and through the brush to the edge of the ravine.

"Dad!" Elspeth gasped when she saw her father lying flat on his back. Fergus flew down and landed next to Jack as Elspeth shuffled down the steep embankment, struggling to keep her footing in the slippery mud. When she approached Jack, she couldn't help but notice the enormous stranglerat lying, bloated and lifeless, a few feet away.

"Are you okay?" she said, kneeling beside Jack while trying to regain her breath.

"I'm fine," said Jack with a wheezing sound. "And the queen? Please tell me you were able to rescue her."

"They did it," said Fergus. "They got her back, safe and sound."

Jack smiled, and Elspeth brushed his thinning hair from his forehead. "That's wonderful news," he whispered.

"Yes," said Elspeth. "But this? What happened here?"

"Just a little encounter with a stranglerat," said Jack.

"We sure showed him a thing or two, didn't we?" said the stick, still firmly clutched in Jack's hand.

"Kevin?" said Gene. "Is that you?"

"Geno!"

"You two know each other?" said Elspeth.

"They're cousins," Fergus explained.

"Well, how do you like this?" said Gene. "So, tell me, Kev. What have you been up to lately?"

"Not much. Things are pretty quiet out here in the sticks."

"Listen," said Elspeth. "I'm all for family reunions, but you'll have plenty of time to catch up on the way back to Banbury Cross. Right now let's focus on getting Jack out of here. Are you able to stand?"

"Not without passing out, I'm afraid," said Jack. "I think I may have cracked a few ribs."

"First you almost lose your foot trying to find me," said Elspeth, "and now you've almost been eaten by a stranglerat? And what's all this about you jumping bail?"

Jack looked at Fergus. "You told her?"

"She was going to find out sooner or later."

"Find out what?" Elspeth demanded. "What's going on?"

"I've been accused of murder," said Jack. "The Muffin Man."

"They think you did it?" said Elspeth. "But that's absurd."

"Of course it is," said Jack. "But they've got witnesses who swear they saw me there."

By now, the others were making their way down into the ravine, each taking a long look at the dead stranglerat as they passed it. "What is that thing?" asked Bo-Peep.

"It *was* a stranglerat," Kevin said. "Before I gave it the beating of a lifetime."

"Gene's cousin," Elspeth explained.

When the brothers had succeeded in dragging Mary Mary down the hill and the entire group was together again, Elspeth explained the situation, saving Jack and his broken ribs from having to speak unnecessarily.

"He's unable to stand," Fergus said. "So it looks like we'll have to carry him."

Cory was noticeably uneasy with this proposal.

"What is it?" asked Winkie.

"Well," he said. "It's just that he's . . . well, he's slightly—"

"Fat?" offered Gene.

"I think full-figured is the generally accepted term," said Kevin.

"But certainly he's not too heavy for you and your brothers to bear," said Dumpty.

"Yes," said Cory. "But if we carry Jack, who's going to drag Mary Mary all the way back to the castle?"

While the question was being considered, their thoughts were interrupted by an odd and rapid clicking noise, as if a stick were being struck against a hollow log in rapid repetition like a jackhammer. While they listened, wondering what might be the cause of it, Mary Mary seemed to know exactly what it was. She parted her lips and sent forth a low, guttural laugh.

"What is it?" Winkie demanded.

"You'll find out soon enough," said the witch. "She's lured by the smell of the stranglerat. But she prefers the taste of humans."

"She? Who's she?" asked Elspeth.

A second later, Elspeth's question was answered by the appearance upon the ridge of a creature that would have looked something like an iguana if iguanas had large spikes running along their backs from the top of their heads to the tips of their tails and were capable of growing to the size of an SUV. Its skin was thick like an elephant's but green and spotted everywhere with what appeared to be large, spongy warts. Its eyes were bulbous and highly active, as was its bright-pink tongue, which shot out rapidly and repeatedly to a distance that nearly matched the length of the animal itself. Each time the tongue flicked out, a fast and rhythmic clacking noise resonated from deep within the animal's throat.

"Oh no," said Dumpty. "Is that . . . the Great Spiny Gleekin?"

"The greatest of them all," said Mary Mary. "Say hello to Sally."

Now that the smell of the stranglerat had led it to the humans, lined up like an all-you-can-eat buffet, the Great Spiny Gleekin, otherwise known as Sally, wasted no time in making its way down the hill, its tongue flicking, its throat clacking.

Fergus took to the air and flew over the monster, taking a swipe at its nose. But this was no stranglerat, and the animal remained unfazed and undeterred as it continued inching its way down the hill.

Cory knelt to allow Winkie and Farrah to climb to the ground. Then he stood and drew his sword. His brothers released their grip on the witch and did the same, taking position alongside Cory, forming a wall of sword and muscle in front of their king and queen.

"Run," said Jack. "By the time it's finished eating me, you'll be out of the Thick."

"We're not going anywhere," said Elspeth. "We're going to fight."

"With what?" said Jack.

"With this," said Elspeth. She reached into her jacket pocket to retrieve the golden pear and was horrified to find that the pocket contained only her house keys. She quickly checked the other pocket to find it empty. The golden pear was gone.

"Krool," she gasped, suddenly remembering the awkward hug. "He's got it. He's got the golden pear." And without it, there was no way for Elspeth to assert control over the Great Spiny Gleekin.

"This is not good," said Dumpty as the beast steadily zigzagged its way down the slope.

"If only you could roll uphill," said Gene.

The animal's pace was incredibly slow, which might have been comforting if anything at all was known about the Great Spiny Gleekin. Whether it had the ability to move much faster than it was currently demonstrating was not known—until it did.

Just like that its movement went from plodding and deliberate to quick and aggressive. With a rapid clicking, it charged forward and its tongue launched forth from its mouth like a frog with a fly in its sights. But this was no frog, and it had much bigger prey than flies on its mind.

Jack screamed as the rough, sticky tongue wrapped around his ankle. He clawed desperately at the dirt, and Elspeth clung to Jack as the Great Spiny Gleekin dragged them both toward its gaping mouth. As they inched closer Jack could feel the animal's hot breath. From this distance, the clicking was deafening.

Cory ran forward, raised his sword, and brought it down, slicing off the tip of the animal's tongue, which instantly retreated back into its mouth where it remained for no more than a second. There was still a considerable portion of the tongue intact, and what was left of it shot out once more and this time wrapped itself around Elspeth's waist.

She being much lighter than Jack, the beast was able to reel Elspeth in quickly and, in an instant, into its mouth she went.

"Elspeth!" screamed Jack. Forgetting all about his ribs, he sprang to his feet just as the beast's powerful jaws came together and then . . . stopped. With Gene in Elspeth's hand, held vertically, the stick had prevented the animal from completely closing its mouth. At least temporarily.

With the animal's jaws out of commission, the three brothers seized upon the opportunity and charged. Their swords met with the creature's thick skin but could not penetrate it. Meanwhile Gene, the only thing keeping Elspeth from being eaten alive, was beginning to bend under the increasing pressure.

"Help!" he cried. "Get me out of here!"

The boys continued hacking at the heavily armored animal, and the witch laughed at the futility of their efforts. There was a cracking noise. It was the sound of Gene beginning to break as the Great Spiny Gleekin easily absorbed the onslaught of swords. Strike after strike barely bruised the animal while it tried very hard to pull Elspeth down its throat and into its stomach. Her terrified screams echoed from its mouth, by now nearly closed.

Jack, with Kevin in hand, gritted his teeth and lumbered toward the animal that was protected by a thick hide over eighty percent of its body. The other twenty percent was made up of its soft underbelly and its large, bulging eyes. With his full weight, Jack plunged the stick into the animal's right eyeball with a sick squishing sound.

With Kevin embedded in its eye socket, the beast reared up on its hind legs and roared with enough force that Gene and Elspeth were catapulted from its mouth a good twenty feet before landing near Dumpty on the soft, muddy ground.

Its abdomen now exposed, the brothers plunged their swords deep into the beast, and the animal howled with each painful puncture. In one final act of self-preservation it dropped to all fours, lowered its head like an angry bull, and charged the brothers with its great spiked head.

It was purely a defensive move, and once the brothers had scattered, the Great Spiny Gleekin turned and ran up the hill. It got only halfway before it rose up onto its hind legs again, let out a thunderous roar, and collapsed.

"Run!" said Winkie as the giant carcass tumbled down the hill. He, Farrah, and Bo-Peep sped off in all directions across the ground made to tremble by the enormous animal that rolled and plummeted nearly as quickly as it had run.

As it fell, its massive spiked tail swept around, brushing the tops the weeds until it met with the small of Bo-Peep's back and sent her sprawling and tumbling.

When finally the Great Spiny Gleekin stopped and lay as still and as dead as the stranglerat, Elspeth ran to Jack, who had collapsed to the ground where he lay in agony. Dumpty ran to Bo-Peep, who lay motionless in a patch of weeds, and Winkie ran to Farrah. Or at least he tried to, but he soon discovered she was nowhere to be found.

"Farrah!" he called, searching the area first slowly and carefully then desperately. "Where is she?"

Dumpty helped Bo-Peep to stand. She was shaken and bruised but otherwise uninjured, and soon she and Dumpty, along with Cory, Rory, Maury, and Elspeth, had joined in the frantic hunt for Farrah, which became suddenly more urgent when it was discovered that the queen was not the only one missing.

"Wait a minute," said Elspeth. "The witch. Where's Mary Mary?"

"No!" wailed Winkie. "She's taken Farrah." He dropped to his knees and buried his face in his hands. "Oh, this is absolutely horrible!"

But if Winkie thought that Mary Mary absconding with Farrah was the worst possible explanation for her disappearance, he was about to find that there was another scenario that was far more dreadful.

Elspeth was the first to see her—only her face, beautiful and serene as ever. The rest of the queen, every bit of her tiny body, was hidden beneath the massive corpse of the Great Spiny Gleekin.

"Over here!" Elspeth shouted. "I've found her."

Elspeth knelt near Farrah, and the others hurried over to find the queen with eyes agape. A faint gurgling sound escaped from her slightly parted lips.

"Hurry!" shouted Winkie. "Get this thing off her!"

The three brothers put their shoulders to the beast, and pushed with their powerful legs, moving the animal just enough so Elspeth could drag Farrah out from beneath it.

"Farrah, my darling. Speak to me," Winkie pleaded. He knelt down beside her and moved his ear close to her lips but heard only the gurgling in reply. "Please, Farrah. You said you would never leave me. You promised me." Then he turned his attention to the others, to anyone who would listen. "Do something. Help her!"

But there was nothing to be done. Her internal injuries were too many and too severe. A small bit of blood appeared at the corner of her mouth and ran down her cheek. And then, the gurgling stopped.

This queen of ours,
She warmed our hearts,
Just like a summer's day.
The beast with warts,
It broke our hearts,
And took our queen away.

Chapter 21

There is a strange hierarchy to grief. Those perceived to have the greatest claim to it are granted the right to express it fully, while others, farther removed from it, are expected to remain strong in order to offer support.

Winkie cradled Farrah's lifeless body in his arms and cried openly. And while Elspeth's heart was no less broken, she fought the urge to fall into a puddle upon the ground. Instead she sat next to Winkie and gently rubbed his back, which heaved with each painful sob.

Likewise, Bo-Peep, Dumpty, and the others could only stand and stare and swallow the pain in their own hearts while Winkie freely gave in to his. That they had all risked so much to save Farrah from the witch and that they had so recently celebrated her rescue with shouts of "Long live the queen" made her sudden passing all the more difficult to comprehend.

And though it may have seemed highly insensitive at such a time, there was another issue that had to be addressed. "Your Highness," said Dumpty, gently as he knelt next to the king. "Forgive me, but it's just a matter of time before another of these creatures picks up our scent. The longer we remain here, the greater the danger."

At that moment, Winkie had no concern for his own personal safety and might have welcomed a quick death and an instant relief from the sorrow that reached to his very core. But, grieving or not, a king must be a leader and there were others to consider.

"Yes," he said. His voice was weak and his eyes dull. "I understand."

For the time being, he remained as he was while Cory, Rory, and Maury went to work, gathering and cutting vines.

Elspeth left the mourning king and returned to where Jack still lay on his back in the dirt. "They're making a stretcher for you," she said. "So don't worry. We'll get you home safely."

"I don't deserve such consideration," said Jack.

"What are you talking about?"

"Don't you see? It's because of me that the queen is dead."

"That's nonsense."

"If I hadn't gone looking for you, I wouldn't have been in need of rescue and she'd still be alive."

"Listen," said Elspeth. "The witch alone is responsible for the death of the queen. If there hadn't been a kidnapping, none of this would have happened." Jack began to protest, but Elspeth stopped him short. "You've been blaming yourself for years for what happened to me as a child. You're no more at fault for that than you are for what's happened to the queen."

"She was your best friend," said Jack. Tears streamed down each side of his face and trickled into his ears. There was something about the sensation that he found pleasant, in a cleansing sort of way.

"I only wish I'd been able to spend more time with her," said Elspeth. "I made as many visits as I could. And of course she could never come visit me in the Deadlands because—"

Elspeth's heart and mind began to race at equally frantic speeds. "Wait a minute," she whispered.

"What is it, Elspeth?" said Jack. "What's wrong?"

"She could never come visit me in the Deadlands because she might turn back into a doll." Elspeth stood quickly and left Jack lying alone and confused as she sprinted back to where Winkie sat, still holding his departed queen while gently stroking that long blond hair that Elspeth had once scissored away.

"King William," she practically shouted.

"What is it?" he said placidly, completely unaffected by Elspeth's urgent tone.

"I have an idea. I don't know, maybe I'm crazy. Perhaps it won't work. But it's worth a try if it might bring Queen Farrah back to life."

For the first time since the queen had been pulled from beneath the Great Spiny Gleekin, Winkie removed his eyes from Farrah's face and looked at Elspeth. "What did you say?"

"I said there's a chance—a small chance—that we can revive her."

Dumpty stepped in between Elspeth and Winkie and spoke sternly to the girl. "What are you doing?" Then he whispered, "What do you mean giving false hope to a man who has just lost his wife?"

"It may be false hope," said Elspeth. "But it may not be. And we'll never know until we try."

"Try what?"

"An operation. A simple operation, but one that can only be performed in the Deadlands."

"You want to take the queen's body to the Deadlands?" said Winkie.

"Only temporarily," said Elspeth. "And with your permission, of course."

"I signed a deal with the devil," said Winkie. "And I faced ultimate evil while risking my life and those of my closest friends to get her back. And now you ask whether you may take her down the well to the Deadlands on the fleeting chance that you can bring her back to me alive once more? I think you know my answer."

Elspeth nodded. "I'd like to leave right away," she said. "The brothers can take Jack to Banbury Cross. Meanwhile, you should go with Dumpty and Bo-Peep to the forest. Down the path from Manuel. Gene knows the spot." She handed the stick to Dumpty. "Wait for me there."

"You mean to travel unescorted?" asked Bo-Peep.

"Fergus will go with me, keeping watch from above."

Bo-Peep looked to Fergus, and he nodded as if it had all been arranged.

Winkie gently lifted Farrah's body from the ground and offered it to Elspeth. "I know it may sound absurd," he said, his throat tightening. "But please take extra special care of her."

"She's in good hands," said Elspeth, and she took the queen in her arms as one would a newborn child, cradling her head in the crook of her arm. "Of course I can't promise anything, you know. But I'll do my best."

"I've no doubt of that," said Winkie.

Elspeth tried to smile in that same reassuring way that Jill would if she were there. "Tell my father I'll see him soon."

She gave one last glance at Jack, and as she turned to leave, Dumpty stepped in front of her. "Elspeth?" he said.

"Yes?"

Though it appeared he had a great deal more to say, all that came out was, "Good luck."

"Thanks." She took a deep breath. "Okay, Fergus. Lead the way."

Another strange thing about grief is that it has the power to partially or completely eliminate fear. When you already hurt as much as you think you possibly can, what is there to be afraid of? And so as Elspeth made her way through the Thick, where any number of vicious beasts roamed freely, she went, not with a sense of dread, but with purpose. Her mission was as narrowly defined as one can be: get Farrah back to the Deadlands and stop at nothing.

Strange sounds and eerie shadows did little to slow her down or to divert her focus, and before she knew it Fergus had led her out of the Thick and back to the friendlier terrain of the forest. But when her guide turned onto the path that would take them past Manuel, Elspeth said, "No, Fergus. Not that way. There's no reason for him to know about any of this. It would break his heart."

"Right," Fergus agreed. "It's okay. There's another path. Follow me."

To the edge of the forest they traveled and out across Torcano Alley. Not even the possibility of being burned alive or falling into a magma-filled crevasse gave Elspeth even the slightest pause. She marched forward as if she were invincible.

By the time they reached the other side and had begun the slow walk up the crumbling switchback trail,

Elspeth's back was numb and her arms ached from being held in one position for several hours. Still, she refused to make movements or adjustments that would jostle the queen in any way.

At the top of the cliff they headed off, not in the direction of Banbury Cross, but instead turned left toward a large, open pasture about a mile across the flatlands. In the middle of the dry pasture sat the well, which amounted to nothing more than a hole in the ground surrounded by a pile of loose stones stacked without mortar and crumbling badly as a result.

Fergus was already perched upon the edge of the well as Elspeth approached. Looking down into the seemingly bottomless pit, he couldn't imagine how someone could take it on faith that to leap into it would not result in injury or certain death. Yet Elspeth had done it on numerous occasions.

"Okay, here we are," she said, not to Fergus but to Farrah. "Now there's nothing to be scared of. It's a bit of a drop and the water's a little cold, but it'll be over before you know it."

Elspeth's greatest concern was neither the long fall nor the temperature of the water but the possibility that Farrah might slip from her hands and become lost in the pitch black at the bottom of the well.

She sighed and rolled her neck, which had become tight again. She sat down on the rocks next to Fergus then swung her feet around until they hung over the edge and down into the dark shaft.

"I'm not sure what you have in mind," said Fergus. "But I hope it works."

"That makes all of us. Now, once I jump in, fly back to the forest and tell the others I made it to the well and that I'll see them soon."

"Will do," said Fergus. "Safe journey."

"You too." Elspeth took a breath, let it out, then inhaled again, as deeply as she was able. This time she held the air in her lungs, then leaned forward and dropped into the darkness.

When she hit the water, her fears were nearly realized when the impact almost jarred Farrah from her grip. She managed to hold on and, with her free arm, she pushed the water aside, propelling herself downward, in the direction of the dim light that grew brighter and brighter as she swam toward it, until its intensity was almost blinding.

She reached out and pulled herself through the portal. When at last she took her next breath, it smelled of mildew and cabbage. Though she had made this very trip several times, at the end of it she was always a bit surprised to find herself lying in a puddle on her bedroom floor. She lay in place for a moment, looking around the room at the vintage posters on the wall, afraid to glance down at her precious cargo. She knew that she was holding either a plastic doll or a tiny corpse, and she took several deep breaths before she could summon the courage to settle it for certain.

"You're dead," she said to Farrah when she finally looked. "A dead, lifeless doll. It worked!"

Elspeth sat up quickly and inspected the doll further, moving the plastic arms and legs along the visible joints. The first part of her plan had worked brilliantly. But there was much more to it than that.

She jumped to her feet and hurried to her dresser, where her new and unnamed fashion doll sat, staring off at whatever might occupy the space in front of its unblinking eyes. She placed Farrah next to the new doll, then picked up the doll and, in no way gently, pulled its head off.

She placed the beheaded doll on the dresser then picked up Farrah. "Forgive me," she said and then, much more carefully this time, twisted and pried her head from her body. Queen Farrah had died of internal injuries, and the only thing that might save her, Elspeth theorized, was a full body transplant.

Elspeth took the decapitated doll in one hand and Farrah's head in the other. The name Frankenstein popped briefly into her own head as she moved the two pieces together and twisted the head onto the neck until it snapped into place.

"There," she whispered. "Good as new. I hope."

She ran quickly to her door, put her ear against it, and listened. She could hear her mother puttering about somewhere in the apartment. She lay down on the floor next to the puddle she'd just made and held tightly to Farrah, outfitted with her fresh, unbroken body, wrapped in a bright yellow dress. "Please," Elspeth said to no one at all. "Let this work."

She closed her eyes, held her breath, and waited. And just as her mind began to drift away, there came a knock upon her bedroom door. Her eyes sprang open, and she inhaled hungrily.

"What is it?" she said.

"Before you take your nap, I'd like to get your opinion on something," said her mother. "I'm going to pick your father up at the airport, and I can't decide which earrings to wear."

Seriously? thought Elspeth. She climbed to her feet and walked to the door. "I'm sure they're both equally lovely," she said.

"If you wouldn't mind taking a quick look."

Elspeth unlocked the door and opened it as little as she felt she could get away with. She peered through the crack at her mother with a different ornament hanging from each earlobe. Delores turned her head side to side several times.

"Well?"

"Definitely the one on the left."

"My left or your left?"

"Yes."

"Your hair is wet."

"I was looking out the window," said Elspeth. "At the rain."

"You shouldn't do that. You might fall."

"May I please go now? I'm very tired."

"Of course. I'll see you when I get back."

Elspeth closed the door and locked it tightly then quickly returned to her spot on the floor.

By now, Winkie had been waiting for hours, wringing his hands and pacing the forest floor. "Are you sure? Are you absolutely certain this is the right place?"

"Gene?" said Dumpty.

"I think so," said Gene. "No offense to the trees around here, but they all kind of look the same."

"And you definitely saw her go into the well?" he asked Fergus for what must have been the tenth time.

"Once again, yes I did," said the owl.

"Then why hasn't she returned?"

"As I understand it, time works very differently in the Deadlands," said Dumpty.

"It's going to be dark soon," said Winkie.

That Bo-Peep with her keen eyesight would be the first to spot Elspeth was not surprising. "There!" she said, pointing with Kevin, whom she'd decided might make a good replacement for her disintegrated fighting stick. "Look!"

Some twenty feet away where once there had been nothing, a girl now lay on the ground, flat on her back, with what appeared to be a blond fashion doll clutched in her hands. For a man with such tiny legs, Winkie proved he could move quickly if impelled by desire.

As Winkie and the others sprinted toward her, Elspeth opened her eyes and heard the approaching footsteps. Soon they would all know whether what she held in her arms was made of flesh and bone or of plastic and paint. Reluctant to look, Elspeth decided on another test and gave Farrah a gentle squeeze that turned out to be not gentle enough.

"Please!" Farrah shouted. "Get this thing off me. It's crushing me."

Elspeth gazed up at the trees and the patches of dusky sky, and, for reasons she didn't understand, she burst out laughing. "She's alive!" she shouted. She sat up and looked at Farrah through the tears in her eyes. "You're alive."

"Of course I'm alive," said Farrah. "But . . . how did I get here? The last thing I remember, I was lying beneath the Great Spiny Gleekin and then—"

"Farrah!" called Winkie, his heart on the verge of exploding with joy and gratitude.

Elspeth gently placed Farrah on the ground just as Winkie rushed up and took her in his arms. "You're back. And you're okay!"

"I'm more than okay. In fact, I've never felt better," said Farrah, as anyone might who's been given a brand-new body. "But what happened to my dress?"

"You did it, Elspeth!" Winkie laughed as he hoisted Farrah off the ground and swung her around in a complete circle. "Once again you've saved the queen!"

"Long the live the queen!" shouted Kevin and Gene.

"Long live the queen," the rest of them repeated.

"Did you hear that?" said Winkie, his eyes locked tightly on Farrah's. "Long live the queen. This time, try and get it right, would you?"

Still unsure of exactly what had happened, Farrah looked at her husband as if he were crazy. "I don't understand."

"Sorry," said Winkie. "It was a joke and not a very good one, I'm afraid. It's just that I'm so happy to have you back."

A tisket, a tasket, a queen once made of plastic,
She fell stone dead, I switched her head,
And now she feels fantastic.

Chapter 22

There was just enough light left in the day to guide them out of the forest, yet not enough to get them across Torcano Alley. While it is generally agreed that traversing such a dangerously unpredictable stretch of land in the dark is simply too risky when traveling on foot, to go by air is another matter entirely.

"You will tell the people that the queen is alive and well," said Winkie to Fergus as he swept his hand in a grand gesture in the direction of Banbury Cross. "And Georgie will arrange a feast like none before. And there will be a parade to welcome her home. Let's see. Am I forgetting anything?"

"Maybe a special tribute to the many contributions made by sticks to our society," Gene suggested.

"Like drumsticks," said Kevin.

"And cue sticks, and yard sticks," added Gene.

"And lipstick," said Kevin.

"Would you two be quiet?" said Dumpty. "This is about the queen, not you."

When Dumpty turned away, the two sticks looked at each other and silently mocked him behind his back.

"Honestly, I wish you wouldn't make such a big deal about it," said Farrah. "I don't feel comfortable with such a fuss being made over me. Please, William?"

"Very well," said Winkie, before offering Fergus a surreptitious wink. "You will tell the people that the queen is alive and well and that she will be just one of many guests at a feast to honor the countless contributions made by sticks to our society."

"Don't forget about the parade," said Gene.

"And a parade," Winkie added. "Now go. There's much to be done before we arrive."

"Yes, sir," said Fergus, and with a quick nod he turned and was off through the darkening sky toward Banbury Cross.

Elspeth found a quiet place upon a log where she could sit away from the group in order to collect her thoughts. She was understandably worried about Jack. The last time she'd seen him, he was lying flat on his back with cracked ribs and dead monsters on either side of him. She could only assume and hope that Rory, Cory, and Maury had gotten him back safely and that his injuries were being properly tended to. Then there was that whole murder business of which she could make no sense.

Farrah approached Elspeth cautiously. She climbed upon the same log and sat down beside her. By this time she had been brought up to speed on her own sudden death and recent resurrection. With no memory of any of it she had to take Elspeth at her word, despite how absurd the whole thing sounded.

"Are you okay?" she asked.

"Oh yes," said Elspeth. "Just thinking about how nice it is to have you back."

"You know, it seems to me that if there's going to be a parade for anyone, it should be for you," said Farrah. "After all, you did save my life. Twice."

Elspeth gazed out across Torcano Alley. She rubbed her sore neck and rolled her head from side to side. "I don't know," she said. "I'm not sure I'm really cut out for this whole fame business. Too much pressure."

"It comes with being a hero."

"I don't mind being thought of as a hero," said Elspeth. "I just don't want to be reminded of it all the time."

"I know what you mean," said Farrah. "For instance, I enjoy being queen because of the opportunities it affords me to help others, but the celebrity part I could do without."

"Speaking of helping others," said Elspeth, "I could really use your help with something."

"Of course," said Farrah. "Anything."

"It's Jack. He's been accused of murdering the Muffin Man."

"The Muffin Man? Who lives on Drury Lane?"

"No, different Muffin Man. Larry. Anyway, there are witnesses who claim Jack was at the scene. Of course the idea that he would do anything like that is ridiculous."

"I agree," said Farrah. "Don't worry. I'll tell William to put Jeremy Nod on it. He's considered the best lawyer in all of Banbury Cross."

"I'd appreciate that," said Elspeth. She gave Farrah a smile that was at least half made of sadness. "You know, it's been a long time since we've talked like this. I've really missed you."

"I've missed you too."

"I'll try and visit more often."

"If you can," said Farrah. "After all, you do have your own life back in the Deadlands. People there need you as well."

Elspeth's smile edged closer to happiness knowing that, at that very moment, her mother was on her way to the airport to pick up her father. Not sure why, but she'd missed him more than usual this time. And though Sheldon would never be as carefree or demonstrative with his love as Jack, there was no denying that he was still the kind of father that many people would love to call their own.

From that point on, they sat in silence and watched as a flickering amber light danced its way through the darkness at the far end of Torcano Alley. At a safe distance, a torcano really was something quite beautiful to see.

Soon after, Elspeth and the others settled in for the night, and in the hours before morning, Elspeth's dreams seemed as numerous as the stars glimmering above her head. There were nightmares about the witch and about Krool. There were dreams that involved being chased by a stranglerat and not being able to run away. There was even one in which she dreamed she woke up to find that everything that had happened in New Winkieland had itself been a dream. When she finally did wake up with the rising of the sun, it took more than a moment to figure out what was and what wasn't real. She wondered if Krool had been there, would he have knowledge of her dreams? And if so, how?

The trip across Torcano Alley was a quiet one. Even Gene and Kevin seemed too tired or traumatized by recent events to make idle chitchat. Farrah and Winkie both rode upon Bo-Peep's shoulders as Elspeth's neck and shoulders were much too sore. As for Dumpty, being that he was half egg on his mother's side, he had neither neck nor shoulders and, even if he did, his recurring vertigo made him a poor candidate for carrying others.

By the time they reached the top of the switchback trail, music could be heard far off in the distance. The celebration, it seemed, had already begun.

"You know, there just aren't enough good songs about sticks," said Gene.

"Maybe you should write one," said Elspeth, who would instantly regret her comment when Gene began to do just that.

"If you've got an itchy spot on your back, go fetch a stick. Yeah, yeah. And if you wanna build a nest, better gather up a mess real quick. Yeah, yeah."

Elspeth had never before had a greater appreciation for music than when they finally neared Banbury Cross and the sound of the marching band successfully drowned out Gene's horrible singing.

It appeared that the entire village was out for the celebration as well as many from neighboring towns. In addition to revelers, the streets were crowded with musicians, street performers, and journalists covering the big event.

When the crowd caught site of Bo-Peep and her royal passengers as they made their way toward the castle, the ovation was deafening. "Long live the queen!" they chanted, as Farrah obliged them with a smile and a wave. This time, Elspeth was more than happy to have at least some of the focus on someone other than herself. Still, she stopped periodically to shake hands, sign autographs, and kiss the occasional baby. When she caught sight of Cory and his brothers she knew her father had made it back okay, but when she spotted Jill moving toward her alone she quickly returned to a state of unease.

"How is he?" she asked. "Is he going to be okay?"

"It depends on what you mean," said Jill, who had obviously been crying. "He's in the prison infirmary."

"Prison?"

"He was arrested upon his return for violating the provisions of his bail."

Elspeth was instantly angry. It was the kind of rage she once felt often but hadn't in a very long time. "Arrgh," she growled. "I feel like breaking something."

"How about a dish or a cup?" said Gene nervously.

"This is unacceptable," she said. "I'm going to talk to the Cheese right away."

"Do you think he'll listen?" asked Jill.

"If he doesn't want to be put through a grater he will."

Elspeth left Jill with the promise to do everything within her power to secure Jack's release and zigzagged her way through the masses toward the police station.

Polly was just putting the kettle on when Elspeth stormed in, slamming the door behind her. "Where is he?" she demanded. "Where's Rodney?"

"Detective Cheese is at the castle on official business," Polly responded, somewhat haughtily. "May I give him a message?"

Elspeth turned without answering and stormed out, taking full advantage of the opportunity to slam the door once more. She fought her way through the crowd toward the castle gate, this time rebuffing any and all autograph seekers and their babies.

Unlike Jill, she was allowed instant and unfettered access to the castle. Being a hero, though a high-pressure business to be sure, did come with its perks. She stopped briefly to stare up at the statue in the courtyard then continued across to the door that led to the Great Hall. There she found Georgie frantically directing the many castle workers and volunteers from the community, who were busy setting up tables and chairs and hanging banners and other things to brighten the walls to match the mood. The mood of the villagers, that is. Elspeth's mood was something else altogether.

"Elspeth!" said Georgie when he saw her, his arms spread as wide as his smile. "You've done it again!"

"We sure did," said Gene.

"You don't look very happy," said Georgie, gleefully ignoring Gene.

"I'm not," said Elspeth. "I need to speak with the Cheese right away."

"Haven't seen him," said Georgie. "I've been a little busy preparing for the feast, as you might imagine. Now, I've got you seated at the royal table, just to the left of the queen. Unless you'd rather sit somewhere else, of course."

"The royal table will be fine," said Gene.

"Actually," said Elspeth, "I won't be staying for the feast, I'm afraid. My father's returning from Florida, and I really should clean my room."

"I see."

"And my other father is in prison, and I must get him out. Before I go, however, I do have a favor to ask."

"Sure," said Georgie. "What is it?"

"It's about the statue."

"Ah, yes. The eyes are too beady. I assure you that will be remedied just as soon as—"

"No," said Elspeth. "It's not the eyes. It's the whole thing. If it's not too much trouble, I would like it taken down."

"What?" exclaimed Gene. "Taken down?"

"You don't like it?" asked Georgie, looking genuinely hurt. Elspeth was unaware that he had been the first to propose the monument and had been the one in charge of spearheading the project.

"Are you kidding? She loves it," said Gene.

"I don't," said Elspeth. "I mean, it was a very thoughtful gesture. It's just that, I think all that bronze might be put to better use. Perhaps as a fountain for the new park. Kids could run through it in the summer."

"I think we should talk this over," said Gene. "Remember, this decision affects both of us."

And it was exactly that which resulted in Georgie's feelings of disappointment quickly turning into warm satisfaction, knowing that if the statue of Elspeth went, so did the statue of Gene.

"I understand perfectly," he said, his enthusiasm sudden and a bit over the top. "And I think melting down the statue and turning it into a fountain is a wonderful idea."

Fame, fame, go away.
Don't come again another day.
Elspeth's not a fan, okay?

Chapter 23

Elspeth continued to stomp through the castle, searching for the Cheese. She started with the more obvious places and quickly moved on to those less likely.

She checked the kitchen, the library, and the woodworking shop, where she found Bo-Peep looking on while the carpenter worked to turn Kevin into a proper Shaolin fighting stick.

"Lookin' good, Kev," said Gene, as the carpenter used a plane to shape Kevin's upper half.

"Whoa, whoa, easy now," said Kevin. "Not too much off the top."

Bo-Peep said she hadn't seen the Cheese, so Elspeth continued her quest. She walked past the entrance to the East Tower and thought it unlikely that the Cheese could negotiate the spiral staircase. Still, she thought that perhaps she could spot him from the tower lookout, so up she went. When she reached the top of the stairs there was Dumpty, surprised to see her.

"Well, hello," he said. "Why are you not celebrating with the others?"

"I'm looking for the Cheese," she said, her rage having by now given way to frustration.

"That's right," said Gene. "And when we find him, the cheddar's gonna hit the fan."

"How about you?" asked Elspeth. "Why are you not celebrating with the others?"

"I've never been one for large gatherings," Dumpty replied. "Besides, I figured I'd be more useful up here. Even without the golden pear, Mary Mary is still a mog. And as long as she has the ability to transmogrify she could be any of those people down there and we'd have no way of knowing."

The idea of such a thing at first caused intrigue in Elspeth and resulted ultimately in a startling realization. "Yes," she gasped, suddenly unable to contain her excitement. "As a mog she can appear as anyone or anything, right?"

"That's the theory," said Dumpty.

"Thank you. Thank you so much!" She took Dumpty's hand and shook it aggressively.

"For what?"

"For saving my father."

Without further explanation, Elspeth left Dumpty dumbfounded and hurried down the stairs and out the tower door where she immediately ran right into the Cheese, who just happened to be rolling merrily by.

"Hey, go easy on the Cheese," said the Cheese before he realized who it was who had just about flattened him. "Hey, Lady E. What's up?"

"We've been looking all over for you," said Gene.

"You put my father back in prison?" said Elspeth.

"I'm sorry, but the cat jumped bail. Gave the Cheese no choice."

"Well, I think I can prove his innocence," said Elspeth. "I'd like to see the file. The interviews with the witnesses. I want to read the transcripts right away."

The Cheese thought about this and could find no reason to object. "If you think you're onto something, then by all means," he said. "You know me. The Cheese stands on the side of justice. I only want to get to the truth."

Detective Cheese escorted Elspeth to the station and provided her with the written accounts from the Baker's Man, Carol Sprat, and several others. Polly offered Elspeth a cup of tea, but she politely declined before sitting down in Detective Cheese's office, where she began intently scanning through the documents, starting with the statement from the Baker's Man. She stopped abruptly when finally her index finger landed upon the appearance of the word "charcoal."

"Yes!" she said to herself as she quickly flipped open

the statement from Carol Sprat and began running her finger along each line until the word jumped out at her once more. "Charcoal!"

She gathered up the documents then stood and pushed back from the desk. She stormed out of the room and thrust the pages beneath the Cheese's nose. "Check this out. Jack didn't kill Larry the Muffin Man. Mary Mary did."

"Mary Mary?" said the Cheese. "That nasty old witch?"

"You have several witnesses who say they saw Jack at the scene of the crime," said Elspeth. "But I can give you at least half a dozen, myself among them, who will tell you that Mary Mary's breath smells distinctly of charcoal, which is how your witnesses describe the person they saw running from the scene, covered in muffin batter."

"Which is a very significant detail," said the Cheese.

"Yes," said Elspeth. "And I can testify, along with King William himself, that we saw Mary Mary appear as a torcano, proving that she's a mog who can take on the forms of other things or other people. People like Jack who, incidentally, smells nothing like charcoal. He smells like garbage."

"I don't know," said the Cheese. "It all sounds kind of crazy."

"Not as crazy as a good man like my father killing the Muffin Man for no reason," said Elspeth.

The Cheese had to agree that Elspeth's theory made at least as much sense as a man with no history of violence committing a crime with no real motive. "It may take a few days to get the charges officially dropped," said the Cheese. "But I might be able to at least get him out of jail based on this. That is, if I can get an emergency hearing before the judge."

Though Elspeth may have held some reservations about being treated as a hero, she certainly was not above using her celebrity status when it came to her father's freedom. "Maybe if you were to remind him that I just saved the queen's life?" she said.

"Twice," said Gene.

"I'll do what I can," said the Cheese.

The next couple of hours were excruciatingly long as Elspeth, Jill, and Gene paced about the castle courtyard. By now the feast in the Great Hall had begun, and the courtyard as well as the streets of Banbury Cross were quiet and well littered with debris. And while they awaited official word from the Cheese, they got something much better. The same door from which Krool had entered the courtyard just days before opened and out walked Jack, escorted by longtime prison guard and honest man, Solomon Grundy.

Propelled by habit and fueled by emotion, Jill and Elspeth, with Gene in hand, ran to Jack and hugged him, a move that reminded all four involved that Jack still suffered from multiple cracked ribs.

"Sorry," said Jill, as Jack winced and nearly passed out from the sharp, searing pain. "I forgot about your ribs."

"That's okay," Jack wheezed. "Just please don't let it happen again."

"I won't," said Jill.

"You have to understand," said Elspeth. "We're just so happy to have you out of jail."

"You're happy?" said Jack. "Imagine how I feel! After all, I can't afford to be going to prison now that I'm going to be a—"

Jill backhanded Jack across the chest, and he doubled over and struggled to catch his breath.

"Sorry, I forgot," said Jill. "Again. It's just that I thought we agreed to tell Elspeth over dinner."

"I'm sorry," said Elspeth. "I don't think I'll be able to stop by for dinner this time. You see, my father is coming home from Florida soon so I really should be going."

"Oh," said Jill, doing a poor job of hiding her disappointment. "Then I guess we should probably tell you now."

"Tell us what?" said Gene.

"Jack?" said Jill. "Would you like to tell Elspeth?"

Jack responded with a pained look and a long wheeze.

"Okay, I'll tell you," said Jill. "The exciting news is, you're going to be a big sister."

A smile sprang to Elspeth's face as she inhaled sharply. "You're pregnant?"

"I am."

Elspeth and Jill squealed and jumped up and down like two girls in middle school when, in reality, only one of them was. "That's the best news ever," said Elspeth.

"For years Jack and I have talked about it," said Jill. "But until we found you it always seemed like we'd be trying to replace you, so it never felt right. Until now."

"I'm so happy for you," said Elspeth. "And for me. I'd like to be here when it's time. Promise you'll send for me."

"I promise," said Jill.

"She and I are going to have so much fun together," said Elspeth, who had already decided it was going to be a girl. "I'll teach her how to play chess."

"And how to kick some butt," said Gene.

If Elspeth had felt torn between her two worlds before, this bit of news only served to muddle and divide her feelings further. By now the sun was dipping toward the horizon, and the shadow from the statue and soon-to-be fountain stretched the breadth of the courtyard.

"I really should get going," she said.

"Of course," said Jill.

"But I'll see you soon," said Elspeth. "I promise." She handed Gene over to Jill. "You should all go and enjoy what's left of the feast," she said. "After all, you're eating for two now."

"So is your father, apparently," said Jill, playfully patting her husband's belly.

"I wish I could join you all," said Elspeth. "Rumor has it that a certain stick is due to receive a special commendation."

"A stick?" gasped Gene. "Is it me?"

"Can you think of another stick more deserving?"

"So then it is me. Whoo-hoo!"

Elspeth smiled at Gene then hugged Jill tightly and Jack cautiously. As always, it felt strange to be heading home yet saying good-bye to it at the same time.

"Take good care of yourself," said Jill.

"I will," said Elspeth. "And you two take good care of each other."

"Maybe start by not hitting me in the ribs," said Jack.

Elspeth watched as her father, her mother, and Gene, the giddy stick, walked across the courtyard toward the door to the Great Hall. Jill looked over her shoulder the entire time, and Elspeth smiled back. It was like a phone call where neither party wants to be the first to hang up.

When they finally slipped through the door, Elspeth turned with a smile and made her way toward the castle gate. She crossed the drawbridge and found Detective Cheese waiting on the other side.

"Hello, Rodney."

"You're not still mad at the Cheese, are you? For throwing your old man in the clink?"

"No," said Elspeth. "I know that the Cheese was just doing his job."

"He was indeed," said the Cheese. "You heading back now?"

"I am. And you? You're not going to the feast?"

"I've got a missing bug case on my hands. Ladybird flew home this morning and couldn't find her daughter, Anne."

"You might want to try looking under the pudding pan," said Elspeth.

"Pudding pan? Sounds a little crazy," said the Cheese. "But I'll check it out."

The two said their good-byes and parted ways, and Elspeth walked alone through the quiet streets of Banbury Cross, past the city wall, and out toward the pasture. When she reached the well, she sat upon its edge and looked back toward the village. It seemed that sitting here she was exactly halfway between her two worlds. She swung her feet around and stared down into the darkness. In addition to being very tired, she felt happiness and a strange sense of well-being as she took a deep breath and pushed herself from the edge and into the abyss.

She came out on the other side as she always had: soaking wet and lying flat upon her back. Elspeth was fond of complaining that nothing ever happened in the Deadlands, but for now it was nice to be experiencing a little bit of nothing. She was quite content to have things back to normal. She took a moment to just lie and listen. She heard nothing and, based on that, assumed her mother and father had not yet returned from the airport. It could be any minute now, and she wanted to make sure she was ready to greet him properly.

A change into dry clothes was the first order of business. She pushed herself to her feet, then walked to her dresser where the head of the nameless fashion doll still sat next to Farrah's old body. She changed her clothes and did her best to mop up the puddle on her floor with a towel. Then she walked to the living room, took a seat upon the lifeless couch, and waited.

Finally, she heard the sound of keys in the lock. The door flew open and in walked Sheldon, lugging a large, lumpy suitcase. His face instantly lost all signs of the weariness of travel when he saw Elspeth. "There she is," he said with a medium-size smile, which was much bigger than the one he usually displayed.

He wrapped her up in a hug that included a pat on the back, a move that Elspeth had always associated with sympathy. "Good to see you," he said, without adding the words "there, there now." Elspeth stepped aside to allow Sheldon room to lug his suitcase into the living room. "And what have you been up to since I last saw you?"

"Oh, not much," said Elspeth. "Just some back-to-school shopping. Got some new sneakers and some new dungarees."

"Dungarees?" said Sheldon with a smile and sideways glance at Delores. "You mean jeans?"

"Yes," said Elspeth. "Jeans. And how about you? How was your trip?"

"Fantastic," said Sheldon. It was a word he didn't use often, and Elspeth could not remember having ever seen him in a better frame of mind.

"Turns out the award comes with a five-thousand-dollar cash prize," said Delores. She patted her husband on the back, not sympathetically, but as a way of showing her pride in him.

"That's great," said Elspeth. "Congratulations. Does this mean we can go to the waterfront tomorrow?"

"It does indeed," said Sheldon. "It does indeed."

The next day's weather could not have been better for such a thing. The air was still and just the slightest bit crisp. Sitting at an outdoor table, Elspeth and her father watched the boats and the tourists and ate fish and chips. They followed up their meal with ice cream in a waffle cone, which they ate as they walked to Pike Place Market. It being Sunday, they found it impossibly crowded but not to the extent that they could not walk side by side and hand in hand past the seafood counter with the giant crab legs and on to the vintage poster shop.

This time Elspeth found nothing that interested her and elected instead to spend her poster allotment on some fresh-cut flowers for her mother and on a small, stuffed crab with the word "Seattle" embroidered across its right claw. It was meant to be a gift for her new brother or sister. Although it wasn't until Elspeth arrived back home that she considered the possibility that the crab, like Farrah, might magically come to life when taken from the Deadlands to New Winkieland. A live crab, she supposed, would make a very poor gift for a newborn.

And as she carried the crab into her room at the end of that perfect day, she was surprised and a bit alarmed to find a small puddle of water in the middle of the floor. Quickly she closed the door behind her and locked it. "Hello?" she whispered. "Is anybody here?"

When there was no answer, she looked first under the bed but found only a large population of dust bunnies. She checked the closet, but that too revealed nothing out of the ordinary. It was only as she placed the plush crab upon her dresser that she noticed something that had not been there before. It was a small piece of paper, folded in thirds.

Slowly, she reached for it, and when she opened it, something slipped out and fluttered to the carpet at her feet. She gasped at the sight of the one-hundred-sixpence bill. Her heart beat faster as she unfolded the note and read the words scrawled upon it.

Dearest Elspeth,
It was such a pleasure seeing you again, and I so look forward to our next encounter. I think I'm

really going to like living here in the Deadlands. So much in the way of opportunity for a person of my unlimited talents and unrivaled ambition. Especially while in the possession of this lovely golden pear.

Until we meet again, please find enclosed a little gift from me to you. Get yourself something nice.

Best regards,
Jonathan Ellington Rutherford Krool

P.S. Pleasant dreams.